John

Urbancik

La Casa del Diablo

For more information, please visit www.darkfluidity.com

ISBN: 978-1-951522-25-4

John Urbancik

La Casa del Diablo

John
Urbancik

La Casa
del Diablo

CHAPTER 1

New Mexico Territory, 1875

After the long ride from the Colorado Territories, Kasper Diehl stopped his horse at the top of a ridge to look down on the last valley before La Casa del Diablo. He wouldn't make it to the town before sunset, so he'd have to find a place to hole up for the night. There wasn't anything in sight but sagebrush and saguaros and the straight line of the railroad.

La Casa del Diablo wasn't the official name of the town he was headed for, but no one he'd met ever called it Grave Hollow.

The sun was still bright, if low and red on the horizon. Kasper had to squint to see. There was no indication of trouble, no sign of ranchers or cowboys or natives. His horse, Rojo, seemed agitated. He didn't want to stop just yet. "Easy, boy," Kasper said. "We've still got some miles before we bed down for the night."

The trail was dusty and not well traveled, so it was difficult to pick out. He could make the next ridge before sundown and camp against its wall. Rain seemed unlikely. He hadn't seen rain since he'd left Denver City, though he'd been in something of a hurry that day. There were men dead and buried in the South Platte

River Valley, and they were the kind of men whose kin might come seeking vengeance.

But justice had been served. Kasper had slept well that night, untroubled, under the stars. Just as he would again tonight, some weeks later. "What do you say, Rojo, can we make that ridge?"

He rode on, keeping the railroad tracks to his south. Those led straight to La Casa del Diablo, but he didn't want to ride into town and announce himself. It had been a journey of some years and many, many miles. He did not want it to end before he found what he sought.

Justice.

Most nights when he slept, he revisited that long ago day much too vividly. He watched again and again as the gang slaughtered his family's livestock, even the newborn calves barely able to stand on their own. His mother pleading. His father trying to scare them off with his Walker Colt. He'd gotten off six shots, but only two had been true.

The gang proceeded to kill every farmhand, his sister, and his mother. When it came time for him, the eight year old boy who had hidden under the house, the leader of that gang pointed a Colt Paterson at his head and pulled the trigger, but nothing happened. "I seem to have used up my ammo," he'd said. "I don't see any call for reloading on your account, now do I?"

That was almost twenty years ago. The gang leader had gone on to do some respectable and disrespectable work that brought him eventually to Denver City and now to La Casa del Diablo.

As Kasper rode, movement ahead interrupted his thoughts. There was a stagecoach, but that wasn't moving. One of the horses was free and making circles. Something was wrong.

He nudged Rojo in that direction, though it didn't take much. His horse knew his mind as well as he did. As he approached, he saw the coachman slumped over, the coach gun hanging limply from his dead hands.

The horses were dead, all but the one which had come free of its reigns but limped poorly, snorting terribly, in obvious pain. It bled from multiple wounds on its flank, evidently buckshot. The other horses had been killed more humanely, but messily, requiring multiple gunshots.

He didn't bother dismounting from Rojo. The coach's horse, hurt and dying, wouldn't be any good to anyone again. He slid his Winchester from its harness on his back and aimed carefully. The horse had suffered enough.

The horse knew what he was about. It stopped moving, seemed to acknowledge and even thank him.

One shot was all he needed.

The sound echoed through the valley. From the stagecoach, it was followed by a muffled cry that cut off quickly.

Someone was inside. Whoever she was, she had a set of lungs.

Dismounting from Rojo, Kasper approached the stagecoach door. Whoever had killed the coachman and the horses hadn't taken any interest in at least its female passenger. He didn't know yet if there might be someone else. He said, "It's alright, ma'am. They're gone."

She gave no response.

"I'm opening the door," he said.

When he opened it, he met the double-barrels of a brand new shotgun. It gleamed, and had maybe never fired a shot. But it didn't waver. It was clearly ready to kill. From that distance, she didn't even have to be a good shot.

The way she held the shotgun, though, suggested she was.

She pushed him back as she stepped into the sunlight. Her clothes were dull and lifeless, meant to hide the fact that she'd had money, but Kasper could see by her hands that she hadn't done a lot of work in her life. The skin was smooth. Pristine might be the right word.

"Who are you?"

"Kasper Diehl, ma'am," he said. "I'm just riding through."

"There's nowhere to ride through to unless you're headed to Grave Hollow."

"I always heard it called La Casa del Diablo."

She eyed him. She didn't lower the shotgun. She held it like a rifle, but he didn't relish the thought of its thunder being the last sound he heard. He raised both hands to show they were empty and said, "If it's alright with you, ma'am, I'll just continue on my way."

"And leave us here, defenseless, in the middle of this damned desert to die?" she asked. "What if there are savages?"

"I wouldn't know, ma'am," he said. "You don't seem quite defenseless to me."

"Put the gun down," another voice said from inside the coach. A man's voice. He poked his head out, showing the silver in his hair and beard. "You said you're Kasper Diehl? I'm Morton Templeton, and this here is my daughter, Della. We're well pleased to meet you, sir. It seems we've been accosted by bandits."

Della did not, in fact, lower the shotgun. She spared an angry glance at her father, then said, "Can you drive the coach?"

"I'm afraid you haven't got any horses left to drive, ma'am."

Della and her father emerged from the coach. In the full light of the setting sun, she was quite the vision. The clothes did nothing to hide her golden hair or sparkling eyes. Morton, on the other hand, though rounded at the edges, had gnarled, leathery hands, and a gold ring on one of those fingers suggesting he was a man of means. His clothes, too, had been carefully selected to pretend otherwise.

"What brings you to del Diablo?" Kasper asked. Della's face twisted a little at that. "I am sorry, ma'am. I mean Grave Hollow, of course."

"Family business," she said.

"We have food," Morton said. "You look like you've been hard riding under the desert sun for some time. Maybe we could share something of our intents as we break bread." He glanced westward, where the sun was kissing the horizon. "You ain't making the Hollow tonight, by any means, and in the morning we can think properly and decide what next to do."

Della finally lowered the shotgun and turned to face her father fully. "I suppose you mean for me to cook the food."

"Best not cook anything," Kasper said. "A fire will give away the fact that you're still alive."

"Of course we're still alive," Della said.

"The men who did this," Morton said, indicating the coachman and the horses, "weren't after us."

"Maybe not," Kasper admitted, "but it's curious that, when they had you, they let you be."

"Maybe they were decent, honest bandits," Della said.

"Honey, there ain't no such thing," her father told her. "Now be a dear and see what we have that we can share with this kind man who, more likely than not, will keep us safe tonight."

CHAPTER 2

Della Templeton lowered her rifle and went back into the coach. She didn't like the look of this Kasper Diehl. He was too rough, all angles, and too handsome a scoundrel. A man riding alone like that in the desert couldn't have good intentions, no matter what Morton might say.

And—*father*, ha! She liked the story. It was better than the truth. There was no way to be sure of how long he'd been following them. Until this gunslinger came riding through, she had been called something else.

But she would never go back to Georgia, so she might as well never go back to her previous name. Della fit her, anyhow. It seemed appropriate for a woman on the frontier.

She did as requested, retrieving hard biscuits and jerked meat and a can of beans. They didn't have much luggage. Didn't need any. They had some money, and some provisions, a few changes of clothes, and not a whole lot else. They didn't need much. They would make do with what awaited them in Grave Hollow.

Morton and Kasper were jawing near the horses. She couldn't hear what they were saying, so she interrupted. "You'll have to eat the beans cold, seeing as I can't start a fire."

"That'll be fine, ma'am," Kasper said, all friendly like.

It didn't take much effort to prepare the plates, but she was used to having plates prepared for her. She used a church key to open the can, spooned beans onto the plates, and set them all prettily in a triangle around what should have been a fire.

She knew the desert could get cold at night this time of year. A fire would've been nice.

When the gunslinger came to take his plate, he acknowledged her with a tip of his hat and a half-smile, like the other side of his face didn't work. It was likely the most he'd smiled in years. She turned to get a better view of anything else. Cacti. Desert brush. The ridge and the railroad. The sun was almost completely descended already.

It was going to be a long night.

CHAPTER 3

Morton Templeton ate with gusto. He always did. Any meal might be his last, so he might as well enjoy it, and might as well get it over and done with as fast as possible so he could get on with the business at hand.

The business at hand tonight was this gunslinger. Gunslingers riding solo through the desert were almost always up to no good. Men riding with other men were almost always up to no good, too. It wasn't as lawless out here as people back east might like to believe, but there wasn't a whole lot of trust going around.

The stranger's eyes were sharp. But they were focused on whatever mission drove him to Grave Hollow. Nothing less than a mission could have carved those hard lines into his face like that. He was interested in Morton or his *daughter*.

Of course, he might as well use the stranger's arrival to his advantage. He needed young Della here to remember just how dangerous the New Mexico territory could be. This was a man who had seen action, and had maybe fought on one side or the other during the war.

"North or South?" he asked.

Kasper Deihl paused in eating. He said, "Didn't seem to be my concern."

"You didn't fight?"

"Not in the war, no."

"How not? Everyone fought." It was a lie, or an exaggeration, but it was an honest question.

After a moment's silence, no doubt considering how to best answer such a probing question, Kasper Diehl said, "War didn't reach where I was."

So that was how it would be. Good. Morton smiled, and forced himself to give a hearty laugh. He would've slapped the man on the back, but thought better of it.

"Why is that funny, *Father*?" Della asked.

"Our friend here," Morton said, "has a way with words, he does."

Finished with his meal, Kasper stood and walked his plate over to Della. "Thank you, ma'am."

"You don't need to thank me for that slop," she told him. "Was hardly food at all."

"I might not have eaten anything, ma'am," he said. "Not before reaching La Casa." He stopped, and didn't finish naming the town.

Morton knew not everyone used the name La Casa del Diablo. Not civilized folk, anyhow. This was a dangerous man. That made Morton laugh again. He was a dangerous man, too.

Just ask the coachman.

CHAPTER 4

With the sun down and the moon a mere sliver in the sky, there wouldn't be a lot of visibility overnight. The last traces of daylight were already fading, and Kasper had no intention to light a fire. He wouldn't have, under any circumstance. Not attracting the bandits, if indeed there were any, was a good excuse to keep them shrouded in the night.

The father, Morton Templeton, took this opportunity to begin a story. "We've been traveling west a few months now. Stopping here and there for supplies and provisions, to do some business when and where we could."

Kasper didn't ask what business Morton was in. There was no indication on the coach of any goods the man might be selling, which meant maybe Della wasn't his daughter so much as a service being offered. It didn't seem an easy way for either of them to make a living. Better to hang a shingle at a whorehouse somewhere in Texas than to continue west.

"Della here, she was born in Georgia, ain't that right, sweetheart?"

"Right as right can be, Father."

Kasper yawned. It was purposeful and intentional, but the old man didn't seem to notice. He went on with his charade. "Ran into a bit of trouble back east," Morton said, "so we're making our way to a new start."

"Strange place to be starting anything," Kasper said. He couldn't help it. As far as he knew, La Casa del Diablo, or Grave Hollow, was a town of some three hundred souls, miners and ranchers who had lost their fortunes and their way, banditos, Mexicans, newly freed slaves. No one came to the devil to make any sort of start. They came to make a kind of ending.

"What brings you this way?" Morton asked.

"Business," Kasper said.

Though he kept his eye on the old man, he wasn't foolish enough to disregard Della. She was younger than him, but maybe braver, a woman wandering the desert with a man such as Morton Templeton. The shotgun might be new and her skin might be fair, but she would've shot him if he'd given her any reason. Of that, he had no doubt.

Della sat in the dark and listened. The moon barely lit the side of her face. She didn't look like she belonged here at all. Maybe she was from Georgia, maybe not, but these two hadn't traveled all that way together as father and daughter.

Somewhere not too distant, there was a campfire, and it likely belonged to whoever had attacked the coach. Kasper got up, drew his father's Walker Colt, and said, "If you'll excuse me a moment."

"We were just getting friendly," Morton said.

Della said nothing. She must've seen the reflection of that fire in his eyes. Without another word, Kasper walked into the darkness, over the hard sand and rock, through the sagebrush and mesquite. As he approached, he saw three men. They sat around the fire passing a bottle of whiskey and spooning hot beans into their gullets.

They were sand-scarred men, the lot of them, but not bandits. Mercenaries. Hired guns. Outlaws, no doubt. There wasn't much difference between these men and the men who had come to his father's farm all those years ago.

He got close enough to be sure there weren't others hiding in the dark. They had five horses lashed casually to a saguaro. It hardly seemed appropriate or proper.

He cleared his throat.

They stumbled to their feet. Their eyes hadn't gotten used to the dark yet, having been trained at each other over the fire, so they couldn't immediately see him. But they knew well enough which direction he'd come from.

Only one of them lifted a gun. It might've been a Colt. It was hard to tell in the dark. It wasn't well aimed. The other two tripped over their words. "We didn't know you was out there." "We was quiet like, but a man's got to eat, ain't that right?"

Only the gunman didn't say anything. Slowly, he trained the weapon more precisely in Kasper's direction. Kasper cocked back the hammer of his Walker so they would all hear it, then announced himself. "Howdy, boys."

"Who—who are you?"

"I'm just wandering through the desert on my horse, and you know what I found? A coach that's been robbed."

"That's horrible, ain't that right, fellas?"

The second man was slowly reaching for his weapon. The third didn't seem to be carrying a revolver, but he had a fairly thick knife in his hands and a rifle on his back.

Kasper stepped forward before it got out of hand. He grabbed the first man's gun barrel and simply snatched it from his grip. "Now, what kind of manners are those?"

The second man lifted his gun, but Kasper got the Walker Colt leveled at his head before he had time enough to pull back on his. "As I was saying," Kasper said, "there's a coach not too far off from here, and I wonder what someone might've wanted from them that they killed the coachman but not the passengers."

"Sounds like they must've had themselves a guardian angel or something," the second man said.

"It makes me think," Kasper said. "To tell the truth, I ain't much of a thinking man."

"Thinking," the third man said, grinning. "It ain't right for fightin' men, is it?"

The first man apparently thought he was outside of Kasper's periphery. He reached quietly for a Derringer he had tucked away somewhere. In the blink of an eye, Kasper moved his father's Walker and let it loose. The crack of the gunshot echoed through the valley. The man cried out, snatching his hand to his chest.

"What you gotta do that for?" he asked.

Kasper didn't answer. Instead, he dropped low, because the second man was obviously thinking of shooting. He didn't like the idea of taking a bullet at this range. That shot went wide, anyhow. Kasper's second shot was precise. It hit the buckle of the man's belt. It was enough of a shock, he dropped the revolver.

The third man held up his hands. In one, he held that knife. Realizing this, he opened his fist to let the blade drop. In the other, he carried a jug. He grinned sheepishly and said, "Kentucky bourbon?" It sounded like a question.

"Now," Kasper said, "I reckon we've got ourselves a bit of a problem. See, I talked to the good folk in that coach, and they claim they haven't got any idea what you stole from them."

"Haven't stolen a thing," the second man said.

Kasper cocked the Walker Colt and kept it aimed at the second man's head. "I'm not asking you." He looked to the hombre offering the piss water whiskey. He could smell it from where he stood, and it wasn't pleasant.

"Wasn't there for no robbin'," the first man said, interrupting. "We were there for—justice."

"Yeah, that's right," the third said. "The coachman. We were after him. A right scoundrel, that one. And a sympathizer."

Kasper didn't ask what that was supposed to mean. "So you didn't rob the coach, and you didn't take a shot at the pretty girl riding inside?"

"Didn't look, didn't care," the first said. "What's it to you?"

"To me?" Kasper smiled. He tried to smile, anyhow. He knew his mouth didn't quite work that way. "I'm just wanting to pass untroubled through the desert."

"We ain't got no interest in you," the third said.

"Now, how was I to be sure of that, without first talking to you fine gentlemen?" Kasper asked. When no one said anything, he asked another question. "Why are you riding with two extra saddled horses?"

The first man grinned. It looked positively demonic in the flicker of the campfire. "Who says we're only three?"

Kasper didn't take the bait. He had watched them long enough to be certain. Those two horses had been meant for Morton Templeton and his daughter.

The second man went for his other revolver. He didn't try to be sneaky about it. He drew, but before he could lift the weapon, Kasper put him down with a single shot.

The first man rolled, scrambling to pull his Derringer. He didn't get a shot off. Kasper's aim was perfect.

By the time he turned toward the third of the hired guns, the whiskey man had run off into the dark.

"I am sorry," Kasper said, not nearly loud enough for the man to hear him. Though he lifted his gun, he didn't fire. It seemed unsporting, and unkind, to shoot a fleeing man in the back. He hadn't ever done it before.

He wouldn't do it tonight.

Instead, he gathered the assorted weaponry around the campfire. The Derringer was old and dirty and might not have fired straight anyhow. The second man had carried a Navy, though it hadn't been well cared for.

The blade was a good Bowie knife, perfectly weighted, sharp, and clean, but also well-used. Kasper liked it. He couldn't leave it to be used against him later, but he regretted taking the weapon like a common thief.

The last, of course, was the revolver he'd picked out of the first man's hands. He hadn't seen anything quite like it before. It was sleek and shiny. There was a horse etched onto the grip. He liked the weight and feel of this, too.

Away from the campsite, he buried the other weapons he'd found. He only intended to keep the knife and the revolver, but he thought the Derringer might go a long way toward smoothing things over with Della Templeton.

LA CASA DEL DIABLO

CHAPTER 5

With all that gunfire, Morton Templeton half expected Kasper Diehl wouldn't survive. But he was unsurprised when the man's figure came walking out of the desert darkness. "See," he said to Della, "there ain't likely to be a man more dangerous than this one."

"You mean, other than you?" she said.

She was smart. And smart-mouthed. "Watch your tongue, *daughter.*"

He almost laughed at the suggestion. She went quiet, not because of anything he'd said but because the gunslinger was returning.

"You found them, then?" Morton asked. He had carefully and quietly removed his Colt Paterson from its holster. That gun had been with him a long time. He kept it close to his hip now and pointed in the general direction of Kasper Diehl as he returned. He would keep it there until he ascertained what the gunslinger had learned.

"Three bandits, yes," Kasper said.

Morton narrowed his eyes. "Only three bandits, you say?" He repeated Kasper's word, *bandit,* because it had sounded like a lie from the other man's lips.

"Did you kill them?" Della asked.

"They won't be any bother," Kasper said, sitting

again where he had eaten.

"What did they want from *us?*" Morton asked, sounding for all the world to be shocked and surprised.

Kasper met his eyes. Even in the dark, a lesser man would feel uncomfortable staring into those eyes. But Morton remained unsure why Kasper betrayed no signs of discomfit meeting *his* eyes.

No matter. The gunslinger had holstered his own weapon and was examining another revolver in what little light the moon lent them. He didn't seem threatened or threatening any more so than a resting mountain lion.

"What's that?" Morton asked.

"A Colt, I believe," Kasper said, "though I can't say I'm familiar with this particular model."

Morton held out his hand. After only a brief hesitation, Kasper handed it over, grip first. Morton squinted to see it better. He turned it over a few times to make it look like he was trying to figure something out, but he knew what it was immediately.

He returned the gun. "What you have here," he said, "is a Single Action Army. I've seen one or two of them, but only recently."

Kasper looked at the Colt like another man might look at a woman. That, more than anything else, gave Morton cause to worry. He had half a thought to just shoot the stranger and get it over with, but that wouldn't mix well with his business or his *daughter*. The presence of the gunslinger might be having the right effect on her.

She sat there quietly, betraying nothing, pretending not to look but fascinated by both the revolver and the man.

"Peacemaker," Morton said, if only to break the silence. "That's what it's called. A Peacemaker. Though far as I can see, it only brings peace to the man shooting it."

Kasper nodded, then said, "If it's alright with you, I'll sleep in the shade of your coach, and the two of you should stay inside. Better for me to be listening to the night."

"Who else might there be?" Della asked. "You killed the bandits."

Kasper shrugged. "There may be more," he said, though he couldn't have believed that. "Coyotes roam these parts. Mountain lions. Rattlers."

"You make it sound more dangerous than it is," Della said.

"Begging your pardon, ma'am," Kasper said, "but I reckon that's the only reason I'm still alive at this tender age."

Morton got up, making a big deal of stretching and yawning. "Yes, we'll have an early morning, I'm sure of it, and still many miles to reach Grave Hollow."

Della seemed hesitant to follow him into the coach. But there wasn't much choice. She wasn't in a position to demand a room to herself. There would be no room service here, no servants bringing her tea and biscuits, no maid turning down her bed. Only cold, rough coffee with the morning sun.

He would've felt better having an eye on the gunslinger overnight, but there wasn't any practical way to make that happen without further arousing the gunslinger's suspicions. He would sleep with the Paterson close at hand.

CHAPTER 6

Kasper Diehl watched the father and daughter climb into the coach, then listened to the night. There was still the third hired gun out there, but it was likely the man, yellow as a daffodil, would only live long enough to run afoul of the local Apache.

He aimed to sleep under the stars in good sight of the coach. He wouldn't stay so close as he'd suggested. There was something about Morton he didn't trust. The man was a liar and probably a thief. And if Kasper was being honest with himself, the man looked to be a killer. He had hard eyes and a steady hand, and he had almost successfully concealed his revolver sitting there in the dark.

Someone else might've argued he'd been preparing to defend himself in case the bandits returned.

Kasper listened to song dogs in the distance. He watched the stars. He noted every movement from inside that rocked the coach. They were not father and daughter, but they weren't husband and wife, either. Everyone in the desert had their secrets. He didn't need to know theirs. He was already going to La Casa del Diablo because of his own.

His mind kept going back to the bandits. Maybe they'd stolen something. Maybe they'd had some other purpose. The sickle moon traversed the night sky, but he found himself unable to sleep. He kept his eyes, not on the desert around them, but on the coach.

Long and deep in the night, the door on the other side of the coach opened. A moment later, Della Templeton stepped into view at the front, her self-proclaimed father behind her. She shot a nervous glance around the side of the coach, but finally seemed to catch Kasper lying on the bedroll stretched over the hard rock of the desert.

"Quiet," Morton whispered. They made their way forward, in the relative direction of the bandits' campfire. It had died out a while ago, but five horses remained. In the dark, when Morton looked in Kasper's direction, without any need to scan the area to find him, his eyes seemed to reflect that campfire as though it still blazed.

Despite the hour, and despite the long road behind him, Kasper knew better than to take that as a trick of the light. Better, perhaps, to let them go about their business, whatever it was. But they seemed likely to run into each other in La Casa del Diablo regardless, so it was best to get things settled between them.

He reckoned on another hour or two before sunrise. Rojo looked in his direction. The horse knew it was too early to be getting moving. He made no sound to betray him.

That didn't mean Morton hadn't heard him.

He had been tempted to think of Morton Templeton as an old man, but he wasn't significantly older than Kasper himself. Sneaking through the desert at night, he seemed as spry and agile as a man half his age. He guided Della with a possessive hand at the small of her back. He owned her, and she knew it.

They went straight toward the horses. The third of the bandits, who had dropped his Bowie knife, stepped out from behind the animals.

"I expected you to be dead," Morton told him.

"I half expected the same," the bandit said. "Man had a clear shot at my back."

Morton finished the statement for him. "As you ran."

"He came with an eye for killing."

"There were three of you."

"I didn't have my gun."

"I told you they were dumb," Della said.

"Hey, don't you be flapping your jaw about me," the bandit said, stepping toward her and raising a threatening hand.

"Enough," Morton said. "Mr. Diehl, have you heard enough to satiate your curiosity?"

Kasper, unseen and unnoticed by the other two present, said, "I might have a question or two unresolved."

"Best they stay that way," Morton said. He didn't bother turning around. He had reason to believe Kasper wouldn't shoot him in the back.

"We're riding into La Casa..." Kasper stopped. Della turned abruptly as he started to say the name, so he stopped. She might be in this situation of her own free will, but she'd been at least coerced into it.

Something in her eyes said she wanted saving. But Kasper had always been too quick to jump to that sort of conclusion.

He finished with, "We've already run into each other. We might as well ride the rest of the way together."

Now that he'd seen the man, Kasper didn't relish the thought of leaving him to go about his business unattended. It was bound to be nothing good. And, while that might be the norm this side of the Mississippi, it wasn't the only way to be. Plenty of men were set about a right and moral path, however they defined that to themselves. Morton Templeton seemed likely to ignore a rational man's definitions of morality.

"You," the bandit said, turning his threatening gesture uselessly at Kasper, "are a goddamn menace."

"That's enough, Bert," Morton said.

"No, it ain't," Bert said. "This man's a murderer twice over, I saw it was my own eyes, and a thief to boot."

"Is that so?"

"That knife was my father's," Bert said.

"You shouldn't have just dropped it and run," Kasper told him.

The man rushed toward him, but Morton leveled a shotgun, the same weapon Della had brandished earlier, in his direction. "I said enough."

Bert stopped, but he had all the look of an enraged bull facing a fence for the first time.

"This is silly," Della suddenly announced. "He's right, *father*, we're all headed to the same place, and I daresay we'll be safer on the road with him at our side than on our trail."

"I won't stop you going," Kasper said. "But we'll doubtless have words once we've both reached Grave Hollow."

"What about my brothers?" Bert asked.

Morton spit at the ground between them. "Brothers?"

"Okay, they weren't my brothers," Bert said. "Not by blood. But by God, shared experiences can make a man your brother just as much as sharing a mother's..."

Morton shot him. From that close range, he exploded Bert's skull and scattered blood and brain matter three yards behind him.

Della cringed, but didn't run.

Kasper pulled his Walker Colt, but didn't feel obliged to defend himself.

Morton ejected the spent cartridge, held the shotgun vertical, and handed it by the barrel to Della. It might have been uncalled for, but Kasper couldn't judge their experiences prior to this moment. It just made it harder to understand what was going on.

"I shouldn't have bothered with the subterfuge," Morton said, turning to face Kasper with his palms up and empty. "You're a reasonable, and I daresay an honorable man. But you must understand, those qualities are rare this side of the desert."

"Which side is that?"

"Aboveground," Morton said.

Della put in, "A corpse can't lie to you."

It was naïve, but reasonable. Kasper didn't want to refute her. Instead, he asked, "What's your business, exactly?"

"Trade."

"What are you trading?"

Morton smiled. "Would you believe souls?"

CHAPTER 7

Della shuddered when he said the word. She hadn't believed it back in Georgia, not even when her father told her the stories, and she'd barely believed it on this long journey west, but now she wasn't so sure. She said, "Enough with the jokes, *father.*"

Morton smiled. It was a big, broad smile, charismatic in the light of day, frightening when she knew the first red line of the sun cracking the eastern horizon was still so far off. Before he could say anything, Della asked, "And what's your line of business, Mr. Diehl? Do you also seek souls?"

The gunslinger shook his head once. She almost didn't see it, but the light of that sickle moon revealed something of the movement to her. She was sure both men saw perfectly fine in the dark, each by the fires burning within them.

"What, then?" she asked.

"I aim to put an end to an injustice," Kasper told her. "You understand what I mean, don't you, Mr. Stapleton?"

"I do."

"I don't," Della said.

Morton Stapleton looked at her and said, "That's because your upbringing made you too dependent upon the sweat of others."

"And whose fault is that?" she asked.

He grinned at her. "Your father's, of course."

He wasn't referring to himself.

Morton Stapleton took a deep inhalation and said, "We might as well have breakfast before we go. Daughter, be a dear and get us a little fire going. I believe we have time for some bacon, biscuits, and coffee, wouldn't you agree?"

She glared at him, but she might've glared at the side of a mountain just as effectively. She glanced at the gunslinger, wondering what might've happened if he'd arrived even one day earlier, then stomped off in the direction of the coach.

She hoped one of those men would kill the other before they ate.

CHAPTER 8

Morton watched her walk away, but kept his eyes on the gunslinger. "I must admit, there's something about you I like," he said.

"Why did you kill your own coachman?"

Morton smiled. "Sometimes, when you're in a position like mine, the men you surround yourself with reveal themselves to be soulless." It might've been the most honest thing he'd ever said. "I suspect our lines of business won't cross once we reach La Casa del Diablo." He used the gunslinger's name for it purposefully. He'd heard it numerous times before and understood the truth of it.

"If Lady Fortuna smiles on you," Morton said, "that Peacemaker may bring you peace, after all."

"I prefer my father's gun," Kasper Diehl said.

Morton narrowed his eyes to get a better look at the Walker Colt. He'd seen many in his days, though it seemed unreasonable to assume he might be able to place this one. "That means your father's gone."

"You might say that."

"What might *you* say?"

Kasper didn't seem eager to answer that. He looked to the sky, crossed himself quickly, and said, "Murdered."

"Ah," Morton said. "So the purpose of your journey is laid bare."

"I trust," Kasper said, "you'll stay out of my way."

Vengeance, justice, whatever a man called it—that was something Morton Templeton understood. He didn't smile, though, because grave business like that rarely brought anyone peace except in death.

Instead, he said, "Let's eat." He took the reins of two of the horses, one each for him and Della, and led them back toward the coach. He didn't bother watching Kasper Diehl anymore. He felt he had a better understanding of who the man was, what he wanted, and what he was capable of—and also the extent of his ignorance.

CHAPTER 9

The road to La Casa del Diablo was never expected to be safe. Kasper Diehl had buried bodies behind him, though most had been left to the vultures and coyotes. He tried to do right when he could, but nothing would deter him from his intentions.

Presently, he found himself wishing for a moment alone with a woman.

Della Templeton kept secrets, but it seemed likely those secrets were guarded more by the presence of Morton Templeton than anything else. And it seemed very unlikely that they were a father and daughter traveling west together.

He didn't know if it was his desire to know the truth that burned within him or a desire to know Della.

So he said nothing. He joined them at the small fire Della had started. She'd gotten some bacon on a skillet and a pot of water into which she'd tossed a handful of coffee beans and salt. She said nothing as she did this, but stole numerous disappointed glances at both men as she worked.

Morton Stapleton had apparently satisfied himself as to Kasper. He had nothing else to say and nothing else to ask.

Kasper, however, found himself thoroughly dissatisfied.

But the man had been right. It wasn't up to Kasper to rescue Della, if she even needed rescuing, and it wasn't up to him to deliver justice for the coachman who had died before they met. He remembered the cries of his mother and sister. His father's dead eyes. The smell of the cattle and the swarm of flies that came after.

The unpleasant memories served to remind him of his intentions and how close he was to finishing the work he'd sworn to complete that day.

It hadn't taken a lot of effort to learn the name of the gang leader. The man had already been wanted for countless other crimes. Damon Rose.

It had never seemed a real name, but the face was just as well known. He and his men had been cheating at cards, drinking and whoring, fighting, and terrorizing farmers and ranchers on both sides of the Mississippi before reaching the Diehl ranch. They'd continued west after that.

It was some years before Kasper had caught up to any of them. Hard men, they were too frightened to talk, but eventually most of them did. They told Kasper everything. How Damon Rose had been the only survivor of a theater troupe taken by savages somewhere north of Oklahoma. How Damon Rose had assembled his men, finding two or three at a time and telling them he needed only one. How Damon Rose had killed a variety of bankers, marshals, cowboys, judges, and ranchers.

They described some of this in great detail.

One even mentioned the Diehl ranch.

Kasper hadn't been too kind about that revelation.

They'd eventually, twenty years after, led to the Colorado Territories. Three months there saw Kasper Diehl closing in on the man himself: Damon Rose had retired wealthy in La Casa del Diablo.

"You've seen Grave Hollow?" Kasper asked.

"Ain't never been this far west in my life," Della said. "But I've seen the place in my dreams."

"It's an ugly town," Morton said. "If the stories are to be believed. Ruffians, murderers, marauders of the worst type."

"What stories might that be?"

Morton shook his head. "The kind meant to keep a certain kind of prospector away."

"You don't have the look of prospectors," Kasper told him.

"And I said nothing about gold."

"Ain't no gold in Grave Hollow." Della said it like it was a well-known and unassailable fact, which Kasper was willing to accept. Gold didn't drive him, and it didn't drive these two.

He still didn't know what they wanted there.

Maybe they were on a mission of vengeance themselves.

Fortunately, Kasper Diehl wouldn't have to sleep on that thought. They were less than a day's ride away. As the sun rose, painting red the outlines of mountains to the west, the pale light of morning gave way to a stark, unforgiving sun. It would be hot today, hot and dry all the way into del Diablo.

Breakfast behind them, Morton and Della loaded some provisions from the coach onto their horses. Kasper didn't offer to help. He didn't know what they would want to take, and he didn't mean to inadvertently discover something they wanted to keep to themselves. Let them have their secrets. He could worry about them, and about Della Templeton, after he'd dealt with his own business.

They kept the railroad tracks to their south as they rode, without undue haste, to La Casa del Diablo.

CHAPTER 10

The sun climbed past its zenith before they came into sight of the town. It sat at the edge of a valley. Something they must've called a river ran alongside the western side of it. Barely more than a trickle, it kept some of the land green and provided water for their cattle and the townsfolk.

Townsfolk was a generous name. They were cutthroats, bandits, and thieves.

Their first view of the town was from above, as the ground sloped down toward the valley. Two main roads crossed at the center of town, one ending at a big house by the river. The congregation of ramshackle sheds and clapboard buildings leaned on each other. Removing any one wall might bring the whole town crumbling in on itself. The mountain to its immediate west rose steep and tall.

Closer, they saw a makeshift gallows where the picked-at remains of two men dangled and fed vultures. The ropes were tattered, but until it broke, coyotes might have a time of getting to the meat, and there mightn't be any left by the time they fell. The long street brought them between an inn and a saloon, outside of which several women in provocative garments smoked and laughed together. But that was a hard laughter, not the kind generally full of mirth. They stopped when strangers rode into town.

All eyes turned to watch them, from inside the saloon or its upstairs windows and from men trudging through the narrow streets. The railroad passed south of town, but there wasn't a station here. The town had come after. Its residents probably saw the railroad as an illicit means of support.

In the days since he'd first come upon the railroad tracks, Kasper had neither seen nor heard a locomotive.

A crow perched upon a weathervane over the church. The weathervane topped a cross that didn't inspire much by way of hope or glory. The breeze through town carried dust, death, and decay.

There was a man with a sheriff's badge. He looked the arrivals up and down with a grave expression, then turned and walked away. Others closed up their shutters. Only the women outside the saloon seemed uninspired to flee, but they also failed to call out to their prospective clients.

"Have you arranged for a place to stay?" Della asked. She had ridden between the two men, as neither seemed willing to be penned between the other two. "I understand the inn has got a clean bed or two."

"I've made no arrangements," Kasper admitted. He never did.

"Good luck to you, then," Morton said, tipping his hat. "Be about your business, and I'll be about mine."

"Where are you staying?" Kasper asked.

Morton merely smiled.

He and Della rode on, without hurry, as Kasper hitched Rojo to a post and entered the inn. It didn't look promising. The innkeeper smelled of weak gin and the interior was as dusty as the exterior.

"I reckon you'll be wanting a bed," the innkeeper said.

"If you've got one," Kasper said. He put down some money on the counter. "Enough for a couple of nights, I expect."

"Three, yes," the innkeeper said, scooping up the cash, "but I'll be needing a name for the book, anyhow."

"Kasper Diehl."

The innkeeper frowned as he wracked his brain for information and knowledge he didn't have. "Should I know that name?"

"No."

That was about all that was needed to be said. Kasper didn't have much by way of belongings and no luggage to speak of. The innkeeper handed over a key to room two, upstairs at the end of the hall. The place had three rooms total, and it seemed unlikely that he was ever full up.

The room was sparse, like the desert itself. Kasper might've been more comfortable on his bedroll in the sand surrounded by rattlers, sidewinders, and mountain lions.

On the approach into La Casa del Diablo, Kasper Diehl had noticed the big house on the western edge of town. Bigger than everything else in town, it either belonged to the local whoremonger or the town's wealthiest resident. Considering Damon Rose's occupations before coming here, he might be both those men.

Kasper went over his weapons, cleaning and reloading them, and checked the blade of the Bowie he had picked up in the desert. With Lady Fortuna at his side, as Morton Stapleton had suggested, he might be about his business immediately and done before sunset.

CHAPTER 11

People on the street continued about their own business as Kasper Diehl walked the length of the road. Mostly, that seemed to involve leaning against posts or sitting on steps and watching what strangers were up to.

It was late in the day, so his long shadow followed behind him. The further from the inn he got, the less apparent the purpose of structures on either side of the road. What might have been gambling dens and whorehouses behind him gave way to anonymous buildings that stayed up only because of momentum. There had been a general store, but no bank and no feed shop, little that he'd expected.

Yet in half of every window, faces stared out at him and followed his progress.

The men of this town—it was primarily men, and not a single child to be seen—were hollow-eyed and rail thin. They hadn't been cleanly shaven in weeks or months, and had likely never been clean. If one got too close, no matter how stealthily he moved, the odor would give him away.

The big house stood at the end of the road as though the rest of the town had sprung up to serve it. Three stories high, it had glass in every window and a fence around the property. It was the only structure not in contact with another and likely the only one whose foundations weren't rotten underneath.

He opened the gate but didn't bother closing it behind him. Either this wasn't the home of Damon Rose, or there'd be at least one dead man inside before the sun slipped beyond those mountains.

Those mountains already burned with the red and orange firelight of sunset.

He climbed two steps to the porch. The wood was old and weather-beaten, but unlike the rest of the town it stood a good chance of surviving a sandstorm. He considered simply breaking through the door, but there was a chance Damon Rose was not inside and that wouldn't be civilized.

Nothing in La Casa del Diablo was civilized.

He knocked twice.

He didn't have to wait long. Della opened the door, looked him up and down, and said, "I reckoned we would see you again eventually, but I didn't expect you to come straight away like that. Come in."

Unmoving, Kasper asked, "This is your home?"

"It's *my* home, Mr. Diehl," Morton said from somewhere behind her. "And that makes it my daughter's home, despite that she's never seen it before."

Della moved back and aside. Kasper stepped over the threshold and into the sitting room. Shelves held books and nautical devices, compasses and sextants and the like, things out of place in the desert.

Morton Stapleton, seated on a big, plush sofa, no longer carried the shotgun but did have that Paterson on his hip. "You look surprised," he said. "I made my fortunes in New England."

"I expected somebody else," Kasper admitted.

"Well, now you're here," Della said, "you should probably stay for dinner."

Kasper shook his head. "No need to put you out," he said.

"If I might inquire," Morton said, "who did you think you would find here?"

Kasper considered telling them everything. It wouldn't be the worst mistake he'd ever made. Chances were, he'd still soon be gone. One of the townsfolk went by, or once used, the name Damon Rose. That man might have watched his long walk through town, but he couldn't possible recognize Kasper Diehl. He wouldn't be aware that the bullets in Kasper's Walker Colt knew his name.

If Morton Stapleton turned out to be somehow acquainted with Damon Rose, things could turn very ugly very quickly. But there was no way of finding the man without saying his name aloud. So he said it. "Damon Rose."

Della seemed confused by this. She looked at Morton, no sign of recognition in her expression.

But Morton Stapleton knew the name. His eyes revealed it, and he did nothing to hide that knowledge. He made a sound that might've been dismissive, might've been half a laugh, but was definitely not appreciative.

Kasper realized his mistake one breath too late. He pulled his gun, pointed it at the man's belly. In the same instant, Della drew the Derringer he'd given her. She had been hiding it somewhere on her person, but when she produced it, the unwavering barrel nearly touched his ear.

"You might want to put that away," she said.

Kasper didn't. But Morton Stapleton, whose weapon was easily within reach, didn't bother reaching for it. "If you're done," he said, to both of them, "I can ease your head, Mr. Diehl. That man and I...are not one and the same."

"How do I know you ain't lying?"

"Put that thing down," Della said again, cocking her gun.

He had entertained the idea that she needed rescuing. This didn't support that assumption. Kasper lifted his hand, letting the gun dangle in his finger by the trigger, then slid it back into its holster. "Are you satisfied?"

"Not in the slightest," Della said.

Morton smiled and leaned forward. "That man...he lived here, one time, but that was a while ago. I didn't see him leave, not personally, but I know he did. He rode west. He gave up on making a life for himself here. Grave Hollow ain't exactly known for its hospitality."

"Neither is he," Kasper said.

"No, I suppose he wasn't," Morton said, nodding. "Della invited you to dine with us. Now, I insist. Maybe, before the night is done, we can get you pointed in the right direction."

"I'm half tempted to just shoot you and get it done with," Della said.

"Now, my dear *daughter*," Morton said. "That won't accomplish much of anything."

LA CASA DEL DIABLO

CHAPTER 12

Morton Stapleton felt at ease, even when the gunslinger had his gun out and ready to shoot. As Della reluctantly lowered her Derringer, Morton felt positively delighted. He wasn't sure there could have been a better outcome.

"The truth is," Morton said, "he was driven out. Unliked and unwanted, even here, in this ugly, barren place. His reputation preceded him, and the townsfolk of Grave Hollow decided there wasn't any place for him here."

He didn't often find himself in a mood for storytelling, but he went on. "He'd come with a couple of friends, two or three of them, I can't be certain. I wasn't here at the time. His friends, the town strung them up by their necks, left them swinging at the far end of this road. You saw the corpses hanging there now.

"As to the man himself, he slipped out of town. He crossed the river. It ain't deep. But he crossed, and entered the mountains, and that was good enough for the folks in town."

"They didn't pursue him?" Kasper asked.

"To what end? They wanted him gone, not dead. They got what they wanted."

"So he might've gone anywhere," Kasper said.

"Might have," Morton said. "But I reckon he didn't go far. See, he was made to run, so he left quite a few of his belongings here. And by belongings, I mean gold." He laughed, though it was short. "So I suppose there's some prospectin' to be done in Grave Hollow, after all, if you're here looking for what he left behind. But you're not a man who rode all this way in search of another man's gold, are you, Mr. Diehl?"

"That's an awful story," Della said. "This is an awful place."

With a look, he stopped her from continuing. He didn't care what she thought of the place. He didn't think much of it, either. There were reasons he hadn't taken residence here.

"I've heard whispers," Morton said, "that he didn't go far. That he's there now, in the mountains, wandering as a ghost, restless and uneasy."

"You mean, he's dead?" Kasper asked. He sounded disappointed. That was the type of thing a man like him wanted to be responsible for.

"Whispers ain't always truths," Morton said. He picked himself out of the chair, yawned with a big show of his arms, and said "I'm famished, how about you?"

"I ought to get back to my room," Kasper said.

"You might do that," Morton said, "but I suspect what you really need is a good meal."

CHAPTER 13

Kasper tipped his hat to Morton Stapleton, in thanks perhaps for the story but not because he trusted the man any more, and flashed Della his best smile, which probably wasn't worth much of anything. He'd said what he'd come to say, so without another word he turned back to the door to step outside.

Opening the door, however, revealed the entire population of La Case del Diablo, or damned near close enough, outside the gate. They said nothing, and had made no noise to betray their arrival. There were easily two hundred men out there, a few women, even the sheriff right up front at the gate Kasper had left open. They were quiet enough that the only sound was the buzzing of flies between them.

The faces wore no true expressions. They might have been corpses standing out there. Occasionally, one or another would blink. One yawned. One brushed away a fly on his shoulder, but that was the most animated any of them were.

Only the sheriff, standing at the gate, seemed capable of breaking his paralysis. He took one step inside the gate, removed his hat, and held it in both hands in front of him. His badge was tarnished and smudged. He grinned, revealing a couple of missing teeth, and said, "You go on and tell Mr. Stapleton I reckon it's almost time."

Della, behind Kasper, pushed the door shut without a word. She had to touch him to do this. Compared to the desert, her body pressed to his back felt hot and her breath more alive than the breeze through La Casa del Diablo. Without moving, she whispered at his ear, "I reckon it ain't time yet, and we ought to sit ourselves at the dinner table."

"Is this going to be a problem?" Kasper asked. He didn't have ammunition enough to fight off a whole town. He wondered what Morton Stapleton had done to earn their derision. Maybe the story he'd told had been true, the townsfolk detested Damon Rose, but had lied about not being that man. He turned. Della hadn't put a lot of distance between them yet, so he kept his voice low. "You seem mighty calm, considering what I just saw."

"And what did you see, Mr. Diehl?" Della asked, putting on her Georgia voice and charm. "A rabble, do you think? Perhaps an angry mob?"

"My daughter reads too much gothic fiction," Morton said.

Kasper turned to face the man. He'd gotten off the sofa and looked to be pleasant and jovial, but he most certainly could not be. "What did you do," Kasper asked, "to earn their ire?"

"*Ire?*" Morton asked. "Nothing, I assure you. They're here because...well, it's a new moon out there tonight, rising in the east when it's ready, and if you didn't notice that's straight down the road and out of town. If I understand these people, and I have lived here for a time else this fine place would not have been waiting for us, they're here to...*bear witness.*"

"Bear witness to what?"

Morton shook his head. "Whatever it is, I'm sure it won't happen this side of midnight."

Kasper stared at the man. Della remained close, that Derringer still hidden somewhere on her person. He wondered what else she had hidden under those clothes. He could smell her, from this close, and though she'd been on the road for weeks and probably months, she smelled cleaner than everything else in this town.

"There's steak," Morton said. "Good, healthy chunks of it, and potatoes, and whiskey if you want it."

"You're going to ignore them outside?"

Morton shrugged. "They're out there. I'm not worried about them."

"There's nothing stopping them from overrunning this house."

"They won't," Morton said. "I heard you talking to the sheriff. Sounds like a rightly civilized man, don't you think?"

Why neither of them seemed to be at all concerned with what he'd seen outside, Kasper couldn't fathom. The way those men had looked at him. Women, too. Vacant. Almost hungry.

"They won't come into this house uninvited, Mr. Diehl," Morton said. "They wouldn't dare."

Kasper leaned to look out the window. There they were, two hundred of them at least, only the sheriff on the inside of the gate still clutching his hat before him like a man intent on contrition, his head bowed in reverence, the red glow of the setting sun washing over all of them like an omen.

The silence out there unnerved him some. He heard no birds, neither hawks nor owls, and no coyotes. The approach of the townsfolk had been in a blanket of utter silence that covered the whole of La Casa del Diablo.

"From the back of the house," Morton said, "we can watch the sun slip down a crevice in the mountains. The house was built on this spot for a reason. For that view, which doesn't happen every day and certainly doesn't happen every new moon."

"Where the sun goes tonight," Della said, "the moon will later follow."

Morton left the sitting room, walking down a hall toward the back of the house.

Della darted in to kiss the side of Kasper's mouth. She smiled, and followed her father down the hall, leaving Kasper momentarily alone in the sitting room.

He glanced out the front window again.

Faces stared back at him, but if anyone saw him there they made no sign.

Kasper followed after Della. The hall wasn't long. Portraits hung on the wall, but they were old and faded and might have portrayed anybody. There was also a chart of an ocean. It didn't look like the Atlantic, but being no seaman, nor having seen an ocean shore in all his life, Kasper suspected he didn't have a solid grasp of oceanic navigation.

The hall ended at a dining room. The kitchen must've been off to the side, through a doorway, but the door was closed and three settings had been set at the table. Morton sat already at the head of the table, which put his back toward Kasper but let him look straight out through the back window.

The view out there was as described. The edges of two mountains descended to create a V straight ahead of them. The red sun was bigger than the sliver of sky still visible and sinking quickly.

There was also the river, which wasn't much of a river at all. Kasper might walk across it without getting his ankles wet. Still, the trickle moved fast over the rocks that made up the river floor.

Della sat at her place, on one side of the table. Another setting had been laid out for Kasper. He'd been expected. Or someone had been.

They intended to eat despite the people outside.

Morton already had cut into his steak and was shoving a forkful into his mouth. "I eat every meal as though it's my last. One of them will be." His Paterson sat on the table next to the cutlery and in easy reach.

Della shot him a look, then cut into her own steak.

No one was visible outside the back window. The townsfolk hadn't surrounded the house. That meant Kasper wouldn't necessarily have to fight his way through them. He hadn't left anything at the inn but money and his rifle, so nothing prevented him from just walking out the back door and disappearing into the mountains.

"I don't believe the stories," Morton said, cutting another small chunk of meat, jabbing his fork out toward the mountains. "I don't think he's dead."

Kasper sat. He didn't have the stomach for food no matter how tender it looked. The other two ate, without urgency, but watching them shovel food into their mouths made him ill. "It's time for what?"

Morton shoved another piece of meat into his mouth and closed his eyes to demonstrate how much he was savoring it. "Ours has never been a civilized society," he said. "Underneath our masks, every one of us wants the same things. Food. Shelter. Recreational procreation." He grinned. "Dominance over the land, our lives, and the lives around us."

Kasper had never given the matter much thought. He didn't start now.

"Some men simply aren't meant to die easy."

"Some men," Della added, "are."

"Isn't my daughter insightful, Mr. Diehl? I would hate to live inside that mind of hers. If you've heard her in her sleep, you know the nightmares that plague her."

"The nightmares are recent," Della said, "and only since you..." She paused. She didn't want to finish the statement, but she couldn't leave it hanging. "Since you came to Georgia."

"I should go," Kasper said. "If he's not in La Casa...if he's not here, then in the morning, I'll push on."

"Don't," Morton said, smiling and nodding toward the back window. "You'll be wanting to see this."

Kasper looked outside. The very edge of the sun had reached the juncture between the two mountains. That last bit of light blinked out in a flash of red and orange. Briefly, the mountains shimmered in the first light of evening. Though the sun no longer shone behind them, and the new moon provided no light, the mountains remained visible for a moment.

When the shimmer faded, those two mountains faded with them, leaving behind a road from the river straight into an ancient city.

There were dozens of structures, all carved straight out of the earth, seemingly dead against the horizon. The other mountains remained. The desert sand and sky remained, But a silvery light fell over the city from the sky.

Morton pushed back his chair as he stood. "My dear," he said to Della, "I believe it's time."

LA CASA DEL DIABLO

CHAPTER 14

The sheriff, still carrying his hat, entered the dining room. He cast his eyes about the room, taking in each of the three of them, settling last on Morton Stapleton before saying, "I reckon it's time."

"Yes," Morton said, nodding. "Yes it is."

The sheriff walked to the back of Della's chair. She shoved one last forkful of steak into her mouth before pushing the chair back and rising. She dropped the fork on the plate, glanced at Morton, and then glanced at Kasper Diehl.

He didn't give her much hope. That wasn't a thing she'd ever had. Even before she left Georgia, she'd known this was what it was coming to. She wished she'd had the chance to get to know Kasper Diehl, or any man, really, more intimately.

But that was not part of what Lady Fortuna wanted of her.

The sheriff put a hand on her arm just above the elbow. He meant to guide her like a criminal. She shook her arm free and said, "I see the way just as easily as you do."

"Maybe," the sheriff said. "But I have been there before."

He didn't make another attempt to grab her.

Kasper Diehl got to his feet. "If there's something I can do, ma'am."

"Always so polite," she said. "I'm...well, forget me, that's the best you can do. Go find the man you want to see dead and make him that way, and leave me to my own fate."

Then she strode out of the dining room, through one the back doors flanking the window that led to the river and the rarely seen city. It had a proper name, but it was unpronounceable, so she didn't even attempt it in her mind. La Casa del Diablo worked fine.

She stole one last glance at the stranger, then stepped outside.

Nights in the desert were often colder than the days, but the temperature had dropped twenty degrees. The city itself was cold. She splashed through the river, the sheriff one step behind her to her left, and everyone else behind them.

Everyone else meant the whole of Grave Hollow. Except for their feet in the river, they didn't make a sound. Not one word was spoken. Not a single one of them coughed or laughed or spit tobacco. They walked with deliberate and silent intent. It made her nervous, which was a stupid thing to be because she already knew how this was meant to end.

She would die.

CHAPTER 15

Kasper rested one hand on the grip of his Walker Colt and even reached into his vest to put his other hand on the Peacemaker. Della Templeton walked out that door and toward the city, followed first by the sheriff then by every other resident of Grave Hollow.

The city they walked to must've been the true La Casa del Diablo. Stories about this place didn't do it justice.

The townsfolk filed past the table, each looking dirty, gritty, scarred, beaten down by the desert. One of the prostitutes walked past him and reached out, stroking the back of his shoulders with her fingertips. He met her eyes briefly and she almost grinned back at him.

The townsfolk wore no expressions. They walked without hurry. They said nothing. Even their footfalls were quieter than a whisper, despite the number of them.

As they walked, Morton Stapleton talked. "I believe," he said, "the man you're after didn't simply disappear. The city you see, it only appears like this one night every...decade, I think, give or take. It's to do with moon phases, and you need complicated mathematics to work out the details."

Kasper didn't look at him. He watched the townsfolk. Some of these men had fought in the war and still carried their weapons and insignia. Both sides. Some were obvious criminals. If Kasper had made a habit of remembering the faces on wanted posters, he no doubt would've recognized a few.

They reminded him of a religious congregation following Della across that trickle of a river.

"But they tell me there are mountain passes that reach that city," Morton said. "I haven't explored those mountains myself. You'll notice the railroad runs far south of this. Wouldn't want to lose a locomotive like that."

Most of the people ignored Kasper. A few glanced at him and a couple stared.

One reached in front of him. Kasper had his Colt Walker out and pointed up at the bottom of the man's chin, giving him only a brief pause. Morton stopped talking for a moment, but the man simply snatched the uneaten steak off Kasper's plate and tore a healthy bite out of it before continuing.

"My guess," Morton said, "is that your man crossed the river and found a way into the city. He's still there."

Kasper had been told Damon Rose came here to retire. It had never seemed likely. The man had spent his life wandering, thieving, carousing, and killing. That type of life generally ended under a boot hill grave.

He looked at every face, trying to match one to the Damon Rose in his memory. Twenty years was a long time, long enough to change a face, but not the basic features of a man. Kasper had assumed he'd recognize Damon Rose. That was why he'd been so surprised to find Morton Stapleton in this house instead.

After the last of the townsfolk walked through dining room, the cook emerged from the adjacent kitchen. The desert-skinned man gave Morton a little bow, then joined the line of people out the door and across the river.

Morton, too, started to walk, on the other side of the table from Kasper. "You are free to find something in the kitchen, if you want to eat," he said. "But I suspect the sheriff of Grave Hollow won't take too kindly to a man who didn't join them on their pilgrimage. If you make the journey, though, I assure you it's a short one, and you may find... *Damon Rose—*" He said it like a curse. "—on the inside."

LA CASA DEL DIABLO

CHAPTER 16

Morton didn't look back. He didn't have to. Kasper Diehl was the kind of man who couldn't resist a mystery. He might have followed just to find out what was to become of Della. He was an honest man, as honest as they're made, but he was driven. Dangling Damon Rose had done the deal.

He didn't turn when he heard one of the doors open and close again behind him.

Crossing the river didn't seem like a big undertaking. It hardly deserved the word river. It was a runoff from the mountains. In a drier season, the riverbed might be as dusty as the rest of Grave Hollow. A flash flood might make the river untraversable, and might've been seen as a sign from God against their intentions.

A chill had settled over this side of the river. It wasn't the normal cold of the desert at night. This cut through to the bones.

Ahead, the two lines of townsfolk approached the city, one of them savagely tearing into the meat from Kasper Diehl's plate. He had risked having his brains splattered on the ceiling, but Kasper wasn't fool enough to miss the fact that every man and woman in Grave Hollow made this journey armed.

On the other side of the river, the road was even

under his feet. Not rock, not sand, it had been carved by hand out of a stone not generally found in this part of the world. He had seen it before, of course. During his time in New England, he had worked on a number of boats, sailing further into the Arctic every chance he got, in search of a particular island that might've only existed in legend.

In one particular coastal town, where the church had been built with this very same stone, he had discovered texts referring to dead but dreaming gods, how they had arrived long ago and slept beneath the ocean.

Long, long ago.

When these very mountains had been under water.

As they walked, the city rose around them. The first obelisks were not more than half the height of a man. Space about ten paces apart, they lined the road and grew in height as he progressed. Soon, those towers rose higher than any structure in Grave Hollow. They were perfectly straight and smooth, all of them, except in places where letters, numbers, and unrecognizable sigils had been carved.

Maybe the sheriff could read those words, but he'd been a resident of Grave Hollow all his life and had probably run through these streets back when this territory was shunned by the local Apache and Navajo tribes.

Without missing a step, Morton said to Kasper, "I'm glad you decided to join us. This is dangerous territory. And I don't mean because of the Mexicans."

CHAPTER 17

Kasper Diehl had seen soldiers walking home from the front lines. The war was over, their bodies were weary, their hearts heavy, and they walked in straight lines, one after the other and silent as the grave, just as the people of La Case del Diablo were doing now.

He realized that name didn't really belong to Grave Hollow, but to this place, where a full moon shone brightly through temple columns, where the ground had been smoothed by endless oceans, where statues of — *men,* presumably — had been carved into columns.

They ascended into the mountains. Ahead, stairs climbed the side of a pyramid with a flat top. The further they walked from the house and that steak dinner, the colder and thinner the air got, the stronger the myriad odors of rot became, and the louder his heart pounded within its bony prison.

Kasper had seen strange things in his time, but this might be one of the strangest. The moon, he noted, was yellower than usual, and its face seemed different.

Up ahead, the townsfolk came all at once to a stop.

Morton Stapleton, however, did not stop. He strode between the two lines of people. Kasper, not here for whatever they were here for, followed him. The procession through the dining room had seemed to take forever. It took much less time for him to follow Morton to the front of the line.

There, Della, the sheriff, and a few of the others stared at the column to the left of them. It was tall. A length of wood had been tied to it at almost ten feet high. It wasn't an expert job, but an exuberant job, using lots of rope to hold the wood in place.

Some of that rope had been saved for the noose.

A body dangled from thick piece of wood, causing it to sag slightly. It wouldn't hold for much longer. The wood had blackened, almost as if burnt, but it still supported the body. Blood had dribbled from a bullet hole between his eyes. The badge he wore said *deputy.*

"I reckon we've got trouble ahead of us," the sheriff said, his voice betraying no enthusiasm, no excitement, no sorrow, and no fear.

"Cut him down," Morton said.

The sheriff turned to one of the other men. Scars crisscrossed his face. The whites of one of his eyes was permanently red, the other filmy and probably useless. He carried a machete. With one swing, he cut the noose. The deputy's body dropped with a heavy thud. The man knelt beside the body, started to cross himself, but stopped.

"And I had thought he was a coward," the sheriff said.

The deputy's hands had been bound to each other. His neck was raw from where the rope had cut into him. It hadn't been a clean hanging. His neck hadn't snapped. He's suffocated, slowly, but when that proved insufficient, he'd been shot once in the head. His eyes were open and stared glassily into the foreign sky above.

The man kneeling there pulled a smaller knife from his belt and, with delicate precision, bent close so he could pop the deputy's dead eyes from his skull.

Della made a sound and turned away.

"You can never know," Morton said, "what lies ahead, but the deputy maybe saw something useful."

"It's good to know, if he did," the sheriff said.

Kasper watched, fascinated and appalled, as the man held each eye close to his own as if examining diamonds he'd found in a stolen strongbox. Then, without warning, he popped one of the eyeballs into his mouth and swallowed it.

A moment later, his own eyes rolled back into his head. His words came broken and jaggedly. "Savages," he said. "Dead. Three dead, two more—three more— five." He clamped his eyes shut and shook his head. When he opened his eyes again, the whites were golden like midday sand. "We've got the numbers, Sheriff."

"They've drawn first blood," the sheriff said.

The man shook his head again. "Not the savages. They—were slaughtered, hanging, dangling, dancing in the wind—" Before the amber completely drained from his eyes, he popped the second into his mouth. It seemed to stick in his throat, and he didn't look like he appreciated the taste. "Do you want to see?"

He asked the sheriff, but the sheriff looked to Morton Stapleton for an answer. Morton looked at Kasper and grinned. "I reckon we owe the dead that much respect. Even if they were savages. What do you think, Mr. Diehl? Will you walk with us?"

Kasper looked at Della as though she might provide a reasonable and acceptable answer. She was looking away, up at the sky, giving him a clear view of her profile and a single tear threatening to fall from the corner of her eye. She wiped it away quickly before it fell, then seemed to notice him looking at her and gave him her back.

"How far?" Morton asked.

The man who'd eaten the eyeballs said, "Not very." He nodded beyond the edge of the road.

Four of them took the walk: the *brujo* guide, the sheriff, Morton, and Kasper. They stepped off the road clear of the hanging wood. The road was slightly raised from the mountains on either side. Cave mouths, mine entrances, and holes dotted the mountain walls. The rock had gone a dark gray, whereas much of the rocks in the desert around them leaned toward orange, red, and brown.

The guide led them in through one of these. It was easy to reach. Hardly required any climbing at all, whereas other mouths seemed unattainable from the ground. Inside, the ground sloped sharply downward, but it didn't go far before opening into a huge chasm.

Moonlight shouldn't have reached into the cave

from behind them, but something gave the place a silvery indigo glow. It was like walking into the very fabric of the night sky. Spiders crawled on the walls, unseen things chittered, and from stalactites descending like teeth from the ceiling, seven corpses hung. Parts of them, at least. None seemed to have all their limbs. They were missing hands, whole arms, even legs. Their eyes were too big to be human and set too far from the center of their skulls, and some had been gouged out. The skins had a greenish tint to them. Dry seaweed dripped from them all.

The guide didn't make any effort to obtain a fresh meal. The sheriff didn't suggest that any of them be cut down. Insects the size of a man's fist crawled over the bodies, feeding and burying their eggs in the soft, rotting flesh.

They'd all been stripped of any clothing. No appendages indicated the gender of any of them.

Kasper had seen many corpses in various stages of decay, but no human corpse he'd ever seen had taken on the color of these.

It seemed like no one intended to say anything, so Kasper offered, "They weren't natives."

"Not native to the desert," Morton said, nodding his head. "And not our concern. Perhaps their gods will show their souls mercy."

Kasper turned and exited the cave. Staying served no purpose. If some of those *men* had been alive when the deputy had found them, they weren't any longer.

Della, standing at the edge of the road, met his eye then looked away, forward, and decided not to wait anymore. She started walking. The two lines of townsfolk went after her, not a single man among them expressing any interest in what might've been found in the cave.

CHAPTER 18

Della walked because she didn't want to know. Her childhood nightmares had taken place under a sky like this one. The moon was too close and too bright, the stars arranged haphazardly and wrongly, and the air felt fragile when she inhaled.

Her father must've been here. He must've told her stories. The pyramid felt familiar. This road seemed to have always been beneath her feet.

She knew before they'd gone into that cave that the bodies they'd find wouldn't be human. Maybe their ancestors had been. But they'd lived too close to the perils of the ocean. They'd taken in too much of that salt.

She suspected each of the men in Grave Hollow, and the women, too, had taken their own lungfuls of the Atlantic. None of this belonged in the New Mexico Territory. None of this belonged anywhere on this planet.

As a child in Georgia, she had seen the ocean. Her father had taken her so she could watch the full moon rise over the water and feel the undertow. She'd told him she saw shapes in the water. People, she said. Sharks, he told her. Sharks and squids and sea monsters. Nothing else.

She'd dreamt of this place before then. She was a child. Her dreams should have been filled with life, not death. If they had come to her relentlessly, nightly or even weekly, she might have gone mad from them.

As it was, she understood madness a bit too well.

She led two hundred souls toward a place of sacrifice. She did this knowing men, or men-like things, lurked in the shadows.

When Morton Stapleton had arrived at her father's plantation, the two men seemed to have known each other.

She'd never known her mother. Had her mother, like so many other sharks, squids, and sea monsters, risen from the depths? Or had her mother already been dead, dead but perhaps still dreaming, when her body gave birth to Della?

She reached the base of the pyramid and climbed. The steps were steep, not meant for human legs, so the climb would prove to be arduous. But a long rest was promised for after.

CHAPTER 19

Kasper watched the files of men following Della to the steps at the bottom of the pyramid and on up. He didn't like it. The sides of the pyramid were smooth. Put one foot off the steps, you would plummet back to the base pretty quick. They were barely wide enough for the two rows of men behind her, but that didn't stop her.

The guide, the sheriff, and Morton Stapleton stepped up behind him and cast their eyes on the top of the pyramid. They were meant to be leading the way, but their disappointment was only an irritation. Nothing would happen until they got up there.

He gave the guide a second look. The man had swallowed a corpse's eyes to see what he had seen. He was a *brujo* of some sort, a witch, a practitioner of dark arts Kasper tried his best to avoid. This whole city, Las Casa del Diablo, gave off bad mojo. Winged things flew overhead, but those weren't any kind of birds he'd ever seen before and they weren't bats.

"What is she to you?" he asked Templeton.

The man glanced at him, smiled, and said, "She's nothing."

"She ain't nothing," the sheriff said. "She's a brave girl, that one."

"What is it she's going to do when she gets to the

top of that?" Kasper had a good idea of exactly what would happen. He'd never seen anything like it before, and avoided dealings with the kind of *savages*—not all natives were savage like this—whenever he could.

The guide said, "She's to wake the sleeper."

A gunshot thundered through the city. It was close, but not from anywhere immediately around them. One of the townsfolk, a man just a few paces behind Della, fell to his side, hit the smooth surface of the pyramid, and slid down. His limbs flailed as he fell, but he was already dead. The bullet had cracked his skull. He left a trail of blood and brain matter leading to the bottom, where he came to a stop and made no attempt to move or even breathe again.

Most of the townsfolk stopped climbing. The guide looked to the mountain wall high to one side of them. Holes and crevices dotted the side of it in a distinctly unnatural pattern. A glint of steel indicated a rifle in one of those places.

The sheriff pulled his gun. From this distance, he had no chance in hell of hitting a target that high and far away from him. He pointed it, searching for a target, but even if he'd found the shooter he wouldn't have wasted the ammunition.

Morton Templeton's hand fell to his Paterson, but he didn't bother to draw it. He picked out the rifleman's perch before the sheriff, then glanced at Kasper. "Ten dollars says you know the name of our shooter."

"He could've hit the girl," the *brujo* guide said.

"If he'd wanted to, he would have," Kasper pointed out.

The guide nodded in agreement.

The glint of the rifle had been brief. The shooter—Damon Rose—had abandoned that hole and probably gone to another. Kasper scanned them for any sign of that rifle, but the moonlight hitting the side of the mountain was weak and definitely in Rose's favor.

"He probably ain't alone," the sheriff said.

To prove the point, three additional gunshots followed, all coming from the mountain wall on the other side of the city. They hit three different targets, again near the front of the line. One went down cleanly. Another whirled, taking his neighbor tumbling down the pyramid with him. Another fell where he stood. He didn't go down the side until one of the other townsfolk kicked him out of the way.

"They've got the high ground," Templeton said.

"They have no other advantage over us," Kasper pointed out.

"The savages," the *brujo* guide said.

"There are at least four," Kasper said. "You should go after those three, up there." He pointed at the in the rock wall that might lead up there. "I'll go after Rose."

The *brujo* guide looked up the side of the mountain next to him. His eyes had returned to their normal color, no longer accentuated by those of a dead man, but he didn't look too anxious to search for a way up the mountainside through those tunnels.

"We could wait them out," the sheriff said. "They'll run out of bullets before we run out of men, of that I'm sure."

"Thunder," the *brujo* guide said, "will attract the savages."

Kasper had a feeling he didn't mean the Apache.

CHAPTER 20

Della knew nothing about the men shooting at her, only that their shots had been fatally accurate so far. The minute one decided to aim for her head, she would be dead.

She stopped climbing to watch the bodies slide down the side of the pyramid. She knew nothing about those men, either, except that they'd been living here a long time and had great expectations of her.

Off the pyramid, she saw Morton Stapleton, the sheriff, the stranger, and another man who hadn't rejoined the procession. She didn't know what they'd seen, but it wouldn't have prevented her from ending up right where she was.

The men shooting at her intended to stop her from climbing.

In all of her admittedly short life, she'd never wasted a moment on cowardice. She wasn't about to fall prey to it now.

She looked up to the apex of the pyramid. She hadn't yet gotten half way. Her legs burned from the exertion, but she took another step.

And another.

The residents of Grave Hollow climbed with her. The gaps made by spineless riflemen hiding in the shadows were immediately filled. Men climbed on either side of her, making her a more difficult target.

The next shot came from her right. The bullet pierced the skull of the man next to her. A spray of blood and bone splashed her face. The man fell into her, but the man behind him caught him before he could drag Della down and threw him the other way. The man stepped up to take his place, knowing the gunmen would likely target him next.

Another shot from the other direction hit the man on her left in the shoulder. The force of the bullet spun him around but didn't immediately kill him. Despite not being dead, he stumbled, and one of the other townsfolk shoved him off the steps and down the side of the pyramid.

Two hundred men and a scattering of women escorted Della. At this rate, there would be none left by the time she reached the top.

Another gunshot ricocheted off the step in front of her. The sound wasn't deafening, but it tore off a small chunk of stone. It was a warning. Go no further. Climb no more. Or the next shot will be the last thing you hear.

She looked back again, down at her *father*. The four men had scattered. She saw one of them, the stranger, reaching an entrance on the side of the northern mountain. Maybe someone had preceded him into that cave. More likely, the others had found a way into the southern mountain.

Morton Stapleton followed close behind the stranger. She didn't know why she wouldn't acknowledge his name. Yes, he was a stranger, but he had a name and no less of a relation to her than her self-proclaimed father.

Other men, at the back of the lines, siphoned off in either direction.

So she sat. The men crowded around her, creating something of a shield, though she hesitated to call it human. They stank of desert sweat and swine and shit and salt. She would have chosen another bouquet for her final scent, had she'd taken the time to consider it.

Not roses, though. She had a good guess as to the identity of at least one of those gunmen. So she didn't entertain the thought of his namesake. Maybe some French perfume like the ones her father back in Georgia had sometimes procured for her. Delicate and refined scents that recalled European society and New England aristocracy.

Crouched in a protective bubble of leering filth, Della waited for what would happen next.

LA CASA DEL DIABLO

CHAPTER 21

If Damon Rose found his way up on the inside of the mountain, Kasper Diehl reasoned he ought to be able to manage the same. The cave he entered first, however, was merely a hole in the side of the mountain leading nowhere. He couldn't see this until his eyes adjusted outside the reach of moonlight.

The next entrance was a shaft that led to an open area, not unlike where they'd found the bodies hanging from the ceiling. Here, the stalactites didn't carry bodies, though they'd been generously coated with an oozing black substance Kasper felt he would do well to avoid. The walkways through the cavern, uneven and probably mostly natural, led to a doorway propped up and supported by stone columns. While the opening might have been there forever, the stones had been put in place by people.

He walked through, amazed at the silvery indigo iridescence that allowed him to see. He didn't question the source of it, though. In his mind, he saw his mother, his sister, and his father watching approvingly from beyond the grave. Their spirits hadn't been able to rest properly for going on twenty years now. Tonight, they would finally find peace.

On the other side of the doorway, a tunnel ascended toward the west. Steps had been carved into the ground, though time had made them brittle and uneven. Halfway up the stairs, the faintest sound made him stop and spin, his father's Walker Colt leading the way.

"I'm not the man you want to shoot," Morton Stapleton said.

Kasper wasn't so sure of that. But Stapleton wasn't alone. A half dozen of the Grave Hollow townsfolk had also followed.

They weren't deep enough in the mountain to not hear the next series of gunshots. One first, followed by two others, and finally a fourth. Damon Rose was not alone, but he had no army with him. Kasper didn't need help, but he supposed the townsfolk at his back would prevent Damon Rose, or anyone else, from sneaking up behind him.

He assumed, at least for the moment, they didn't intend to shoot him. If they had, they would have already.

"I want him," Kasper said. "I get him."

"We all want him," Stapleton said. "These good people have been waiting a long time for tonight. They're not going to let some delusional criminal sabotage their plans. They won't let you, either, for that matter, but at present your interests and theirs are aligned."

Kasper narrowed his eyes. "What, exactly, are their interests, anyhow?"

"We should move," Stapleton said, "before one of Rose's bullets finds a home in Della's corpse."

The men behind him grumbled. No words, precisely, but a general chorus of agitation and eagerness.

Kasper didn't offer any response, but continued up the steps. The steps were wide, not actually made by any man but reinforced by people who came before them. Long before Damon Rose.

The steps rose for a while, then doubled back and continued to climb in the other direction. The stairways weren't entirely straight or even. They weren't level or consistent, and because of the ways the paths twisted, they likely weren't climbing straight up the inside of the mountain, but they did eventually reach an opening like a window that looked down on the city in the valley.

At this height, Kasper was just a little higher than Della and the top of the procession of townsfolk, but east of Damon Rose and nowhere near as high. He saw more of the city from here. It continued in straight lines from the pyramid's base in four directions. East, the road led straight back to Grave Hollow. Every other direction contained stone buildings, some of them five, six, even seven stories tall, none reaching the height of the pyramid at the city's center. Just west of the pyramid, there was a square clearing before the structures began. Many of those structures had glassless windows.

Figures looked out from some of those windows.

It was hard to say people, because the shapes were wrong. The eyes were too big and too far apart. None seemed to have hair of any sort, neither on their chins, their heads, or even their eyebrows. They were too distant to see clearly, but they reminded Kasper of the corpses they'd found in the cave.

Stapleton came up behind him and looked outside. "They haven't shot her."

Kasper had noticed that and ignored it. He gestured toward the figures visible in the nearest of the buildings.

"Natives," Stapleton said. "They're in the mountains, too." He gestured at the openings in the southern mountain. Three gunmen hid in holes on that side, but creatures with green eyes looked out through some of the others.

Creatures. Not men, not women, no longer just figures. These were close enough to make out more details, but there were few details to make out. They were not all a single color, but they were all various shades on the spectrum between green and brown. Some looked wetter than others, but they all appeared to glisten when the moonlight hit them.

When one realized it had been noticed, it receded from the moonlight into thick shadows.

"We'll run into one eventually," Stapleton said.

"One should've run into Rose already," Kasper said. "Yet he's still taking shots at Della as though time answers to him." He pulled himself from the window and continued ascending.

CHAPTER 22

Morton Stapleton spent another thirty seconds at the window trying to ascertain the distance Della still had to climb. She wasn't halfway up the side of the pyramid. He had expected to run into the natives, but he had also expected to overwhelm them with iron and lead. He hadn't anticipated Damon Rose still being alive.

The local Apache and Navajo and whoever else lived out this way had avoided this part of the mountains since before the white man came to the Americas, though they told stories of young men losing themselves on vision quests and returning a few weeks later aged twenty years.

Those stories had helped him find Grave Hollow. The town had already existed. The sheriff greeted him personally. When it turned out they had similar ideas of what needed to be done, Morton had gone east to find a man he had fought beside in a war.

A man whose unique daughter had already dreamt the dreams of sleeping gods.

The townsfolk crowded behind him. They were anxious. Grave Hollow had existed in the shadow of La Casa del Diablo since its first new moon. They served the ocean gods, the mountain gods, and the sleeping gods. Morton knew they recognized his usefulness, but he also knew, when they finally decided to turn on him, he would be hopelessly outnumbered.

He relied on their silence to be an indicator of their intelligence.

They had breathed in the exhalations of sleeping gods so long, they'd lost the will to proceed. If Morton hadn't already been in possession of maps from his whaling days, and if he hadn't already studied in that basement in Providence, they would never have marched into this ancient city. They would never have found anyone with the right blood. They would have continued to subsist on the unfortunate rabble who made it their way. After tonight, they would be elevated above all other men.

And they would have Morton Stapleton to thank for it.

CHAPTER 23

At the next window, Kasper Diehl paused again to get his bearings. He'd ascended about twenty feet. His angle was different. If he had his rifle, from here he had a clear shot at Della despite the men crowded around her. They weren't any real protection. If Damon Rose and his men wanted her dead, she'd be dead.

Stapleton, huffing a little, finally reached him.

"You see what I see?" Kasper asked.

Stapleton gave a glance. "It's a clear shot."

"They're higher than this," Kasper said. "They could take her any time they want."

"They believe she's a victim," Stapleton said. "It's a rescue."

"A victim of what?"

Stapleton shrugged his shoulders. "Men like you spend their lives finding victims to rescue. Looks like Damon Rose has a similar heart."

Kasper refrained from putting Stapleton out the window. The descent would be quick, and long enough to be fatal.

Across the way, in another window, he saw one of Damon Rose's men. He wore a black hat that hid his eyes and a thin, scraggly beard that desperately needed the attention of a barber. He held his rifle casually, not preparing to take another shot. He looked across at another window, someplace Kasper couldn't see but was just a bit higher and deeper west, waiting for a signal to continue firing.

There was a good chance Damon Rose had moved, or was currently moving, to another position. None of his men would shoot without his order and he wasn't there to give it. He might be seeking higher ground, or he might be doubling back to meet Kasper and the men behind him.

He must've known they were coming.

From here, Kasper had a better view of the top of the pyramid. It was still above him, but there looked to be a flat surface at the top, an altar of some type.

He also saw movement in one of the windows across the way. Directly behind one of Rose's riflemen, one of the townsfolk, not one Kasper recognized, sneaked toward him and slowly drew his gun. The interior structure must be different in the other mountain.

He raised and cocked the gun. He might've said something, or the sound of the gun gave him away. The rifleman turned abruptly, likely drawing a revolver of his own but Kasper couldn't see it.

Grave Hollow got off the first shot. The rifleman's head split open to decorate the wall behind him. A good, clean shot, it had surely done the job, but the townsman stepped forward, toward the dead man.

Something moved behind him.

It was one of the figures. In relation to the townsman, the figure was easily one or two feet taller. It moved with grace, and apparently with stealth, because the townsman appeared in the next window and prodded at the dead man's chest with the tip of his gun.

Shadows swallowed the figure before he stepped out of view of the window.

"One of the natives?" Kasper asked.

Stapleton merely watched.

The townsman turned at the last minute. The figure grabbed him by the jaw and lifted him off his feet. The townsman fired three, four, five times, emptying his revolver but apparently never hitting his target. When he dropped, the figure still held his jaw in his hand-like appendage.

It was hard to read the expression of a man missing half a face. Pain distorted it. But surely, that was fear, something Kasper hadn't expected to see on the face of any of these townsfolk. The men of Grave Hollow had seemed to be without all emotion, even fear. When their neighbors fell dead down the side of the pyramid, they merely climbed up to fill the gap like good little soldiers.

It had all been a bit unsettling.

The fear didn't last long. The figure — creature — threw the man's jaw aside, then reached down and tore the pipes of his throat out through his neck. He tossed these aside, too, but that was enough to steal the man's life.

From behind the creature, other townsfolk opened fire. They must have been far enough behind him to allow the creature to get between them. There were at least two of them, though Kasper couldn't see because they hadn't yet reached the window. Either that, or one man emptied revolvers in both hands.

The creature turned, disappeared from the first window and passed quickly behind the second.

"I reckon they must've hit him at least once," Stapleton said, "but it didn't seem to slow him down any."

"I'm not sure it's a him," Kasper said, "but I agree. Let's avoid those, and get the man I came for."

Stapleton didn't respond to that. Kasper didn't care if the man agreed. Whatever the residents of Grave Hollow intended to do, Della clearly wasn't being taken against her will. She'd led the damn procession this far. She could handle herself.

Kasper hadn't spent his life looking for victims to rescue. Stapleton was wrong about him. He'd spent his life trying to make enough right to balance the wrong Damon Rose had done. Once Rose was dead, buried or not, there wouldn't be any more need of balance. He could settle himself down somewhere, maybe find a woman to love, buy a few head of cattle, and live out the rest of his life in something resembling peace.

From the window across the way, one of the townsfolk came flying. He pin-wheeled his arms but didn't make a sound as he fell. He landed with a wet thud not too far from the spot where the deputy had been swaying.

He pulled his father's Walker Colt and continued up the steps. He felt more comfortable with the weapon in his hand. Damon Rose might be around the next corner. So might one of the *natives* living here in La Casa del Diablo, even if bullets wouldn't do him much good against one of those.

LA CASA DEL DIABLO

CHAPTER 24

Della looked up to the mountain on her right after a man came flying out from one of those openings. There had been some gunfire, but none of the townsfolk went tumbling down the side of the pyramid. She scanned the other openings for faces or the glints of moonlight hitting rifles.

She did the same on the other side. She caught a glimpse of Kasper Diehl at one of those openings. Gun in hand, he'd paused to look down at her.

For a moment, despite the distance, their eyes locked.

Lady Fortuna had brought them here for entirely different reasons. He could have his revenge for all she cared. She took a breath, sighed angrily, and stood. No more hiding, and no more stalling.

She resumed climbing.

Townsfolk on either side moved with her. A few got in front of her on both sides, but they couldn't flank her as she rose because the steps weren't really wide enough for three people. They seemed hesitant to touch her.

One, in fact, was a woman, one of the prostitutes from town. To Della's knowledge, the only women in town were prostitutes. She looked at Della with a grave expression but offered a weak smile.

They were too much the same. They just traded their bodies in different ways.

Della smiled back at her. Her legs ached from the climb. Every step seemed steeper and more difficult than the last. She saw the end of the stairs ahead of her, though.

As she climbed, she felt the blood inside her veins. It tingled and burned and made a chaotic map of her insides. She tried to shake the feeling, but as she neared the top of the pyramid it became more pervasive. And more perverse.

No shots came from any direction. Della reached the altar at the pyramid's peek. The top was flat and not much larger than a stagecoach. The stone table there had been etched with ornate arabesques. The intricate designs resembled the maps inside her. They would catch her blood. After that, she didn't know exactly what to expect.

Morton Stapleton should be with her. He had the words. And he had the knives.

The table was a step down from the apex. She took that step. The townsfolk circled around the depression but didn't enter, so that six men stood facing each direction, one of them being the prostitute.

She had been a pretty blonde girl, but the hard desert life had aged her beyond her years. She might still be in her teens, but she wore scars, visible and invisible, that suggested a certain strength and hardiness never found back in Georgia.

Della must've had a bit of that herself, now.

She circled the table, running her finger along the abstract etchings. Some of those curving rivulets circled around each other numerous times. On each side, facing each direction, a single spout spilled to a drain on the floor. The blood would then fall into a cistern. Below that, she didn't know where it would go.

But she had a good idea of what slept and dreamt within the pyramid. She didn't remember her childhood dreams, not explicitly. She remembered shadows because she'd dreamt of only shadows. She'd seen this place, this road, and this pyramid. She had seen the natives.

They waited. From the top of the pyramid, she could look past the legs of her human shields and see natives watching from windows in buildings and the sides of the mountains. This city had been carved into the mountains, cutting through it in what must look, from above, like the shape of a cross. The pyramid dominated the center. In one direction, the road would lead back to Grave Hollow until sunrise. After that, she didn't and wouldn't know.

Trembling, she stopped circling the table at its eastern edge and looked back. That little river was beyond sight, so she saw nothing of Grave Hollow, the New Mexico territory, and especially not Georgia.

She imagined her father looking back. He knew the date. He had always known the date. He had told her a man would come for her one day, a man who might be another father but would never be a husband. Once upon a time, she had hoped for just such a thing:

a husband to whisk her away from all the nightmares, a man who might've stood up against Morton Stapleton and carved out a third eyehole with a bullet.

"You'll go west," her father had told her more than once. They were the first words she ever remembered hearing. "You'll go west, you'll see an undiscoverable ocean, and maybe you'll meet your mother. You'll see her eyes again for me, and you'll know them because they'll be like your eyes."

From the top of the pyramid, Della saw where the ocean had been. Countless ages ago, before man ever walked the desert, this had all been underwater. In the east, she saw the sigils of sharks and squids and sea monsters carved too large into the road to have been seen while walking on them.

CHAPTER 25

Kasper Diehl reached the top of the stairs. From here, tunnels went in three directions. There wasn't a window, but he pressed forward, west if his orientation was correct, which should bring him to the opening where Damon Rose had fired his rifle. The way forward looked to hug the outside wall of the mountain, but it wasn't perfectly straight.

He paused a moment to let Stapleton catch up to him. The older man needed a moment to catch his breath. The townsfolk trailed behind him.

Kasper gave him a grin. "I admit, I ain't accustomed to crawling around in the dark like this." He only said anything to give Stapleton a moment to catch his breath. He didn't much like having the man at his back, but that was better than leaving it open for Damon Rose, or one of those natives, to come up behind him.

Stapleton took the moment's respite to look down the other two tunnels. Up this high, they were more roughly hewn from the rock. The dim illumination seemed to come from the rock walls themselves, as though glowing fungi stretched through the veins of the rock like ore.

In the moment's pause, he realized there was a slight variation to the intensity of the light. It pulsed, gently, as if to the rhythm of a heart.

He'd waited long enough. As Kasper stepped forward, he heard a gunshot.

It came from outside the mountain wall at his left. A few seconds later, a second gunshot followed. One more, then silence.

There was no point in rushing forward. He didn't know where the next window would be. He only knew his gun wouldn't change what had already happened.

By the time he reached the window, a line of townsfolk followed behind Stapleton. He had slowed his progress on level ground because he didn't trust it. At any point, a hole might open up in the side wall that allowed Damon Rose to step out and start shooting. The window came first.

Della Templeton had finished her climb. She stood next to a table at the center of a depression at the top of the pyramid. He looked down on her from here, but not by much. It didn't look like anyone else had dropped, but a group of them stood around her like some sort honor guard.

"She's special," Templeton said behind her. "I should be there with her right now."

"You should," one of the anonymous townsfolk said behind him in a flat monotone. There was no emotion, no belief, nothing driving the words, but Stapleton reacted to them. He took a sharp breath, sighed slowly, and said, "You go about your business. I won't interfere. You have your vengeance, and you'll be doing me a favor." He turned to walk back.

Kasper said nothing. Vengeance was his mission, not anyone else's.

The townsfolk pressed to the sides of the mountain tunnel to let Stapleton pass, then turned and followed after him. The natural arcs of the tunnel, which were slight, were enough to hide them from view before they reached the stairs and began their descent.

They moved in nearly perfect silence.

When he was sure he was alone, Kasper took another look outside at Della. She seemed perfectly sure of herself, but he wondered if she needed saving from herself. He had no trust for the man calling himself her father, he suspected the Grave Hollow sheriff only wore the badge because someone had to, and he wondered if some of those townsfolk weren't descendants of the natives that peered out from their various windows throughout the rest of this unexpected city.

He sensed a hesitation in his step.

But the weight of the ghosts, his mother and his sister especially, drove him forward. Let the townsfolk have their secrets.

Not far further, he found the window where Damon Rose had been perched when he'd started shooting. A handful of spent .44 caliber cartridges made it obvious.

He might still be close.

Kasper watched behind him as well as ahead. This was unfamiliar territory. He preferred the open desert and sun-scorched rocks over the damp, dim, unnatural walls around him. Too close, too tight, and too dark, they almost suffocated him.

Listening for any sound, he heard nothing.

Looking outside again, he found Della looking straight back at him. Did she seem anxious? She gave him a smile, a real one, an honest smile that said more to him than any of the words she'd used in the few days they'd known each other. She had come this far, but she didn't know what was next. Or she knew what was coming and didn't like it.

Kasper didn't much like it, either.

He looked forward. Thus far, he'd seen nothing to suggest Damon Rose could've circled back around behind him. The slower Kasper progressed, the more time he gave the man to get away. The ghost of Kasper's father tugged on the Walker Colt, pulling it forward, urging Kasper to get on with what he'd come all this way to do. No woman, no matter how beautiful or wild, could divert him from twenty years of suppressed rage.

"You know, they intend to kill her," a voice said from the darkness ahead.

The voice of Damon Rose. Twenty years on, Kasper recognized the cadence, the tone, but not the intention. He almost sounded noble.

Damon Rose continued. "I reckon you don't want that to happen any more than I do."

CHAPTER 26

The descent was easier than the climb. Morton Stapleton made good time and the townsfolk fell out of sight behind him. They were a strange, quiet lot. Always had been. The first time he'd come to Grave Hollow, he walked straight into the saloon, swept a table clear, and laid out a map without a single word spoken until the barkeep met his eye and asked, "You want beer or whiskey?"

Alone, surrounded by a dim iridescence, Morton went past the windows with barely a look. Nothing changed. Della, good obedient *daughter* that she was, had reached the altar. There was nothing else for her to do until he got there.

Grave Hollow, itself, was not an old city, but the people that populated it had become a part of the place. Maybe they'd eaten too many of the local beans. They came out of the earth dry and dusty here. Local chili peppers added flavor, but maybe stole a little bit of their souls.

They had become languid. Expectant. Because they slept too close to dead, dreaming things. Because an ancient ocean existed somewhere underground. A prospector must've tapped into it some decades back. Generations of hollowers.

Not all the residents of Grave Hollow were born

there. Others had been drawn to them, trapped like flies, and changed.

Changed though they might be, they would've waited forever if necessary for someone like Morton Stapleton to arrive. Someone who had seen the books and heard the stories. Someone who had uncovered old and otherwise useless maps.

That New England town had been much the same. They hadn't wanted to let go of their relics, but in the end, when they could've skewered Morton and scooped out his intestines to appease their gods, one of the natives had risen from the ocean waters. Reeking of sea and salt, it touched him, laying a slimy hand on his chest, pressing down hard enough Morton thought it would shatter his ribcage.

When it backed away, the townsfolk had done the same. Morton's flight from that town was witnessed by almost three hundred souls in complete, utter silence under the light of a full moon.

That odor had infiltrated his dreams and nightmares. It wafted through La Casa del Diablo, but quite suddenly it became overpowering.

Morton stopped his decent.

The native stepped out of darkness. Its feet squelched on the ground. They were surrounded by desert, but the local natives subsisted on what they found in the ghost of an ancient ocean and the tendrils of it that still reached for the surface.

He had to look up to see what should have been its face. Whether those were actually eyes there, it was hard to say. Its arms and legs were humanlike, but there was no indication that it knew how to use them. Gills ran down the sides of its throat. They wheezed quietly when they opened to inhale. Its breathing rhythm closely matched Morton's.

"I brought everything," Morton told the native. He had no reason to believe it understood him or had any way to respond. He spoke with disdain, not out of desperation. "I even brought the girl. *The* girl. Do you know how long I had to wait for her to be old enough?"

The native lurched one step closer and raised its arm. It moved with speed, if not fluidity. Out of its element, it had no intention to remain any longer than necessary. It touched Morton's chest, the same place the other had touched so many years ago when he'd been prone and vulnerable.

He was neither of those things now. He could have stepped back, raised his Paterson, defended himself.

The native touched him, inhaled deeply through its gills, then drew back into the shadows.

Behind him, a half dozen of the Grave Hollow residents saw this and stopped. Whatever they had believed to this point, even after their journey into La Casa del Diablo confirmed those beliefs, they now had to content with the fact that their dark gods had touched Morton Stapleton.

Had touched and chosen him. Twice, though they didn't know that.

Morton grinned at them and shrugged. When they emerged from the cave just off the road to the pyramid, half of those townsfolk hadn't made it. They'd disappeared in silence. Not lost. Taken. Sacrificed. Devoured by the darkness.

Morton paused to catch his breath again and look up to the altar at the top of the pyramid. From here, he saw no details, and didn't see Della at all. The men surrounding her, though, he saw clearly. They played their roles as best they could.

On the other side of the road, the sheriff and the *brujo* guide emerged alone from the other mountain. Whoever had gone into the darkness with them had not survived it. The sheriff's pallor appeared starker. The *brujo*, however, seemed somehow bigger.

Morton realized, then, that the sheriff had been a newcomer to Grave Hollow given the badge because someone needed to wear it. The *brujo* guide, however, wasn't merely a resident. He was a descendant of the natives, crossbred maybe generations ago.

In a way, that made him closer family to Della than Morton had ever claimed to be.

The three met on the road. The sheriff said, "There won't be no more trouble from them."

Morton nodded. He glanced up the side of his mountain and wondered how long it would take Damon Rose and Kasper Diehl to kill each other.

CHAPTER 27

Kasper Diehl saw well enough in the cave's darkness. Though he heard the man as if they were next to each other, he saw no sign of Damon Rose or anyone else. Just to be sure, he said, "You're Damon Rose."

A silence followed. "I reckon I was."

"You robbed and stole and kill't your way across the west," Kasper said.

"And you're Kasper Diehl," Rose said. "You caught up with some of my men in Denver City, and before that in Oklahoma, Kentucky, and Iowa."

Kasper nodded.

"I made a living," Rose said. "Only way I knew how. Only way I know. I ain't proud of what I done, but I ain't about to wear any shame over it. You would've done the same."

"I didn't."

"Only because I made you different," Rose said. "I gave you another way to go."

Kasper bristled at that. The man believed that, by slaughtering his family, destroying his ranch, and leaving him alive at the last minute only because he couldn't be bothered to load fresh bullets into his gun, he'd done something of a good deed. "Then you know why I'm here."

Kasper's father's Walker Colt felt hot in his hand. If it could be anxious to get on with things, it was. But if Rose saw him, Rose could also pull his trigger the moment Kasper started to move. He sounded close, just ahead of him, but there was no bend for Rose to be hiding behind and no other tunnel branching off in any direction.

He didn't much like the idea of finding Damon Rose only to fail in the final minutes of his own life. He couldn't bear the thought of facing his father's ghost and having to admit he hadn't been able to finish the job.

"That your father's gun?" Rose asked.

"It is."

"You've carried it with you all these miles." Rose sounded genuinely impressed. But he said it in a way that implied it had been a wasted effort. "Do you know where we are?"

"La Casa del Diablo," Kasper said. "The house of the devil."

"It's a hellhole, that's for sure."

"It's about to become a grave," Kasper said. "For one or both of us."

Rose laughed. "I can't let you do that, Mr. Diehl. I'm in need of your help."

Kasper nearly laughed. He did laugh, it just didn't sound like mirth. "I don't reckon I'm inclined to help you with anything except dying."

Rose sighed. "I understand. It's—almost admirable. But there's more at stake than you and me."

"Always was."

"More than a family farm," Rose said. "I'll be honest, I've been doing this a long time. I've crisscrossed the country. Survived by my wits, you might say, and by my guns. This here's a special one. I've had it a few years now. Took it off a soldier who thought he'd make a name of himself if he could bring me in. I think the reward money amounted to a mere five hundred dollars at the time. Always thought I was worth more than that. But it won't be enough to get me, or you, through what's coming, if they're allowed to finish what they're attempting. If that girl is what I think she is."

Kasper glanced to his left. He couldn't see through the rock wall, with the window a few steps behind him, but he knew Rose meant Della Stapleton, standing now at the apex of that gray pyramid.

"You see things, when you're a travelin' man like me," Rose said. "You learn things, and they ain't always pretty things. All I ever wanted was a girl to keep my dick wet and a glass of whiskey to keep my throat from drying out. Never thought that was too much to ask for. Now, I went and got myself some knowledge, and I ain't none too pleased with it."

Kasper glanced behind him. Morton Stapleton, and the townsfolk who had followed him, were back there, but none of them mattered. Even if Stapleton came running back up those stairs, the gunplay would be done before he got here. And there wasn't much chance of that, anyhow. He and Stapleton had tolerated each other, but there had always been the chance they'd end up drawing guns on each other.

Might still end that way.

"I want to save the girl," Rose said. "And I need your help to do it."

"Why do you think I'd be inclined to help?"

"You came here with them. You must've seen they're not—right."

"Nothing in that town was right," Kasper admitted. "That includes you and me."

"Indeed, it does," Rose said. He sounded amused. Resigned.

"Why do you want to save the girl?" Kasper asked. "You don't even know her name. You ain't never seen her before. She followed you here, not the other way around."

"I don't care a whit about the girl," Damon Rose said. "I'm only concerned about where she spills her blood."

CHAPTER 28

From where she stood, Della couldn't see down the side of the pyramid, but she got a sense through the rustling of the townsfolk that something was happening. When she tried to get up from the platform, on an even level with the men—and one woman—standing guard on four sides around her, they refused to give her the space she needed.

Maybe they thought they were protecting her from the riflemen. But she suspected they were keeping her in place, and that Morton Stapleton, maybe with Kasper Diehl and the sheriff, climbed the side of the pyramid.

The people on those steps already had to shift their positions in order to accommodate the additional men. The steps were wide enough for two, not for three.

With Morton climbing, that might mean the threat from the riflemen was over, but it might simply mean the time had come. The moon, full over La Casa del Diablo, shone overhead. It looked gray and vibrant, but small. It made Della feel small. The vastness of all that space around it, and all the stars, made her aware of her own insignificance.

Which directly opposed the beliefs of every man in Grave Hollow.

They followed her into La Casa del Diablo, up the side of this pyramid, and to this sacrificial altar because they believed something about her was, indeed, significant.

She touched her Derringer. Insubstantial though it might be, she could kill a man with it. She'd never had reason to, but the day Morton Stapleton arrived at her father's plantation in Georgia, she knew such a day would come.

As Morton climbed closer and the end of her days on this earth came nearer, she wondered if she'd ever get a chance to pull that trigger. As small as that bullet was, it was not insignificant. Not to the person whose body it entered.

She could drop one of the twenty-something men standing around her now, but none of the others would care.

Finally, a hole opened up, and Morton Stapleton stepped into view. He paused there a moment, appearing to anyone at Della's level as a god. She knew better. He looked down at her and said, "I feared one of those bandits might've gotten you."

Della shook her head. "You did not."

He gave only the slightest shrug as he stepped down to her level. She moved away, to another side of the ornate table. The sheriff followed. He, too, took a moment to look down at her. The shine in his eye was nothing like reverence.

The *brujo* guide came last. He looked at her, too, but didn't pause to do it. He seemed capable of anything. A thin line of blood, or some other liquid, was still visible under his lip. He had eaten a corpse's eyes to see what the man had seen last. Why he deferred to Morton Stapleton, she couldn't guess.

The three men circled around the table until, with Della on the south side, they occupied the four cardinal points. The table, however, was not a compass. It was meant to ceremonially divert blood to the cistern below, to wake the dead, to end the dreaming.

Not anyone's blood would do.

Hers was special. Unique. Because her mother had been unique.

She'd never known her mother. The woman died giving birth to her. It had been a prolonged, bloody affair, according to her father, involving much shouting and multiple deaths.

"Your sister was born first," her father had said. "Your sister took three breaths, the midwife told me, and only three." He'd hurried to have the elder child buried because her countenance might be enough to drive a man mad. She had retained too much of her mother's features.

When Della asked about her mother's features, or her sister's features, her father rarely gave her any details. "Beautiful," he would say. "Beguiling." Those weren't useful descriptions. They never gave Della an impression.

The only thing she really knew of her mother came from her own dreams, childhood nightmares that generally faded fast. She had forgotten the tentacles and the teeth and recalled only her mother's angelic voice, eyes blue as a winter sky, and black hair that flowed like shadows in the night. She'd wondered how much of that was true.

Now, atop this pyramid, those dream images came back to Della with greater detail than she'd ever remembered. Tall, of a dark complexion, she hadn't been of Mediterranean stock, but maybe from that sea itself.

Della's father had once, and only the one time, called her a mermaid, but he'd embarrassed himself and spent the rest of the day locked in his study in conference with bankers and farmers, and even servants. Anything to keep away from his daughter, a child of maybe seven at the time, who had innocently said something about swimming across endless seas.

Della frowned.

She didn't want a flood of memories. Now, she wanted to hear her mother's voice. Just once. It didn't matter what she said. She'd never truly heard it.

Morton untied the small, tight pack he'd kept strapped to his back since before arriving in Georgia, and slung it onto the table. Unrolling it revealed a series of iron implements that made Della's flesh go cold. Binders, clasps, and rope; scoops, a frightening knife, and a saw meant to cut through her bones.

CHAPTER 29

Kasper Diehl was not a man who rushed into a thing. His pursuit of vengeance didn't begin at the age of eight. If he put a bullet between Damon Rose's eyes this very moment, he would feel justified. He still couldn't see the man. The unnatural light must've bent funny inside the caves. If he aimed by the sound of the man's voice, he shouldn't miss.

If the caves obscured his sight, they might also distort his hearing.

He said nothing. He nodded, on the off chance Rose had a better view of him, then took a step back. He didn't have to go far, and he made sure to not turn his back on his opponent. He had walked just beyond the window. Now Rose's words made him want to get another look outside.

At Della Stapleton.

She stood on one side of that table. She wasn't alone. Stapleton, the sheriff, and the *brujo* guide were there, too, and maybe twenty-five men over and around them. They looked out, perhaps scanning for riflemen or other threats. Like Damon Rose. But maybe not the natives.

The natives and the men of Grave Hollow must've had years to become familiar with each other. That didn't make them friendly, but it might at least mean they worked toward the same goal.

"You see what they're about to do," Damon Rose said. "You see why I can't risk shooting her directly."

"I can't say I do."

"They want to use her blood," Rose said, "to awaken the sleeper."

The *brujo* guide had used that same word. Sleeper. Against his better judgement, Kasper asked, "What's that?"

"From what I gather, it's big and old and maybe built the earth around it to sleep."

"That's—impressive," Kasper said. He didn't have anything else to say there.

"It's a kind of religion," Rose said, "but it ain't like no God I've ever sent a man to see."

Kasper's eyes were drawn to a glint of metal in the moonlight. Something in Stapleton's hands.

"He's got a knife."

"Then I reckon we're too late," Rose said. "You might as well shoot me. Spare me this particular hell."

Kasper glanced into the darkness of the cave. The light did do strange things with what he thought he saw. The cave itself seemed to waver as his eyes adjusted. It was darker in the cave than outside, but only because of the moon. That light seemed as untrustworthy as what was inside.

Della looked up at the side of the mountain. She, too, had seen the nature of Stapleton's tools as he laid them on the table between them. She had seemed to know what she was doing. But now she looked like a trapped coyote.

Even from this distance, Kasper saw it in her eyes.

Terror.

The reality of what she'd set out to do had finally broken something inside her.

Without warning, she ran forward, away from the steps. She tried to dive over the side of the pyramid. But six men stood on that ledge. Though she knocked one over, one of the others caught her.

She wasn't going anywhere.

Kasper said to Damon Rose, "Give me your rifle."

LA CASA DEL DIABLO

CHAPTER 30

Damon Rose stepped forward quickly, without a word. He didn't give Kasper the rifle. He stepped into the opening, nudging Kasper aside to do so, lined up his shot, and fired.

The crack of the rifle roared like thunder inside the mountain. It rebounded and echoed, and in response, a high-pitched keen resounded from within the mountain. Either the mountain itself reverberated with the sound, or it was the natives within.

If it was the natives, there were a lot of them.

Rose's shot was perfect. He hit the skull of the man who'd caught Della Templeton. They tumbled together over the side of the pyramid.

Damon Rose pulled back from the window and returned the rifle to his back.

Kasper took a step back to get a better look at the man. The twenty years had not been kind to Damon Rose. Scars crossed his cheeks, chin, and forehead. One eye was glass. Marks around the eye suggested how he had lost it, and that it hadn't been a recent wound. The white of the glass eye seemed dim, but the colors in the iris were oversaturated. It didn't look even close to real. Assuming it didn't affect his aim, it probably gave him an advantage against an enemy.

Indeed, Kasper gave Damon Rose plenty of time to

draw that Colt Patterson. It was the same gun he'd used to kill Kasper's father, the same gun that he would have killed Kasper with had there been ammunition enough for one more shot.

Seeing the gun, even the hilt of it hanging on Rose's hip, sent a surge of anger rising up from Kasper's stomach. Before he had time to think, Kasper grabbed Rose by the throat, pushed him back against the rock wall, and, having drawn his father's Walker Colt, pressed the barrel under Rose's throat.

"Pull the trigger," Rose said. "Your thirst for vengeance burns inside you. Kill me and put it behind you. But do it fast, because the girl is still a threat and the good folks of Grave Hollow are not going to let her go that easily."

Kasper hadn't fired immediately. Rose had said things that made him hesitate. He felt no degree of sorrow or pity for the man. Forgiveness, no matter what the preachers might have espoused, was not on the table.

"I won't go that easily, either," Rose said. Their faces were so close, the stink of Rose's breath curled the stubble under Kasper's chin. He had drawn his Paterson and had the weapon pressed against Kasper's balls.

"I'll go," Rose said. "But what happens after? I don't think you'll live long enough to suffer, not with the sacrifice they're intending to make."

"Tell me," Kasper said. "Tell me about the Sleeper."

CHAPTER 31

At the last minute, and probably too late to save herself, Della ran. She tried to push past the wall of humanity that protected her from the riflemen. Too late, she realized they also penned her in and kept her from fleeing. She surprised no one.

The men standing on the edge of the pyramid prevented her escape. They caught her. One man and the one woman standing guard, though she didn't quite have her hands on Della right away. The man held her fast, pushing her back. The woman grabbed her by the arm to pull her.

Then, with another gunshot, the man's skull exploded. Bits of brain matter and skull shrapnel exploded with a cloud of blood. He went immediately from pushing to falling, and Della found herself drawn away from the sacrificial altar and Morton Stapleton's implementation.

They fell. The headless man pulled her, so initially she slid down the stone pyramid with his body as a sled. The woman fell behind her, either pulled or of her own accord.

The pyramid's steep slope meant once she started going down, there was no way to stop. The stone wasn't entirely smooth. The rough edges sheered cloth and flesh. When something cracked loudly, Della wasn't immediately sure it wasn't one of her bones.

Probably the dead man's.

They tumbled over each other. His blood left a long, haphazard trail to the bottom of the pyramid. Della was drenched in it. She checked her bones. She felt sore, and found a few scratches and maybe some deep cuts, though it was hard to be sure how much if any of the blood was hers. Both hands and her right leg hurt from the fall, but she extended and contracted her fingers and bent her ankles. Nothing appeared to be broken.

Not true of the corpse she'd fallen with. Aside from the head shot, a bone protruded from his thigh. Something leaked out of the center of the bone in addition to the spray of blood, but already he seemed to have lost most his blood and there wasn't enough left to spurt.

Della got to her feet. Gray pyramid dust had ground into her long dress and blouse, both of which had been shredded but not to the point of immodesty. She brushed herself down. She'd jammed the fingers of her right hand pretty good. She might not be able to shoot a gun except with her left hand, which meant she might have trouble with her aim. She suspected the bruises would be bright and colorful in a day or two, albeit immodestly scattered about her person.

She looked up the side of the pyramid. The woman who had fallen after her had, in fact, gotten caught up about halfway down. She stared sightlessly down at

Della. Perhaps one of the bones that had shattered during their descent had been the woman's skull.

Beyond her, from the top of the pyramid, the sheriff frowned and Morton Stapleton laughed. The sound barely reached her, but she saw it well enough.

He laughed because there was no place to go.

Della might go around the sides of the pyramid, but the north and south faces descended straight into the sides of the mountains. There might be tunnels, but it seemed unlikely that she'd be able to traverse that distance with the ground that steep. No matter which side she chose, she'd have to get past all the townsfolk of Grave Hollow, which seemed an impossibility.

If she went deeper into the city of La Casa del Diablo, she would have to defend herself against the natives, the outlaw Damon Rose, her self-proclaimed father and the sheriff, all the townsfolk, and even the infuriating Kasper Diehl.

No option was good.

Worse, at street level again, she saw the buildings on this side of the pyramid were occupied. The glassless windows in those buildings resembled those in the mountain, except some of these were at street level. Figures watched her from some of those.

She didn't know much about the natives. She couldn't anticipate surviving an encounter with one of them. A half dozen, further down each of the roads around her , had come out onto the street. She could make it to the square, but that would bring her deeper into the city, not out of it.

This side of the pyramid smelled like the ocean. That brought Della a small degree of comfort. She knew it shouldn't, but some part of her remembered or knew something that had been kept hidden from her.

Something she'd maybe suspected.

Something Morton Templeton's arrival in Georgia had suggested was true.

She looked up again. Templeton, the sheriff, and their guide were gone.

CHAPTER 32

Damon Rose stared back at Kasper as a man who knew he wouldn't live to see sunrise. The glass eye centered his face, making everything else fall out of proportion. "I ain't never seen the Sleeper," Rose said. "Reckon no one has. But those people down there, those people from Grave Hollow, they've been—waiting on it. Waiting a lot longer than you or I have been here. And by here, I don't just mean in La Casa del Diablo, I mean kicking and breathing.

"I came here to rest. To relax. To do a little sleeping of my own. I'd heard tell of the town a long time back, how they built the train line alongside it but refused to stop because of the locals.

"They said locals. The men in Grave Hollow call 'em natives. They don't mean the Navajo or the Apache. You must've seen 'em by now."

"I've seen something," Kasper admitted.

"They got a guy who will cut the intestines out of your brother while he's screaming for them to stop and—eat them. Gives him sight, he says. And the sheriff, he said to me they don't like my kind."

"I reckon you won't find many do," Kasper said.

Rose nodded. "Might be, I've earned that. Don't matter now. The *brujo*, he told the rest of 'em the time was now, the *girl* was on her way, that Stapleton was true to his word. They knew he would be. The only thing they didn't know was what to do about me and my men. There were four of us that rode into town. My brother, they killed him first. They strung Ollie up at the entrance into town, strung him up alive and let him die in the sun with them vultures picking at him, coyotes jumping at him.

"Don't know how long it took for him to finally die, but I could hear his cries from up here in the mountains for at least a week."

"What did he do to deserve the hanging?" Kasper asked.

"Not a goddamn thing," Rose said.

Kasper nodded. It wasn't entirely true. Ollie, and everyone who rode with Damon Rose, had earned their nooses, but that didn't mean he'd earned it here.

"Me and Willie, we ran past the big house and over the creek, and the path through the mountains led us here."

Kasper shook his head. "There were at least three shooters on the other side of the valley."

"We weren't the only men to run from Grave Hollow," Rose said. "Or the only men to find our way to La Casa del Diablo."

He'd reached a pause in his story. He pulled a cigarette from his pouch, struck a match, and took a long inhalation. His eyes focused beyond Kasper and the inside of this mountain. But he didn't seem to be wasting time recalling the good days when he was rustling, thieving, and killing.

Kasper's fists tightened reflexively at the thought. The effort needed to draw his father's Walker Colt would be minimal. Even if Damon Rose was both looking at and seeing him, Kasper could still get the shot off without giving him a chance to respond.

"Before that," Rose said. "Before the good folks of Grave Hollow decided they wanted to read the insides of me, they told me about the Sleeper. They didn't want money, they said. No interest in gold. And I knew damn well some of those men, they had been riding the same damn trails I rode. They wanted to wake the Sleeper and bring an end to all that. An end to—inequities, I think they said. An end to sorrow and pain and the burdens of existence. They said one of the Sleepers, it slept here, in these mountains, under a pyramid old as the mountains.

"When I asked why they didn't just shoot off some guns to wake it with noise, they said it dreams. It shapes us in its dreams. And only the taste of another dreamer's blood could wake it."

Kasper didn't have a word to respond with, but he made an involuntary guttural sound.

"I didn't buy it, either. But those boys could drink, and when they got into their whiskey they liked to talk about how their witch man had heard tell of a girl whose mother was a Sleeper. She slept through the fuckin' and she slept through the birthin', and their friend Stapleton had gone back to Georgia to collect her."

Kasper shook his head. "It's hard to believe you believed any of that."

Rose nodded once. "I ain't saying I throw in with the superstitious or the god-fearin' folk, but the things I've seen in these mountains—changed me."

Kasper almost laughed at that. It must've shown, because Damon Rose added, "I ain't sayin' I'm changed in a good way or a bad way, but I ain't likely to sneer at a man making claims about water and wine. I've seen men walkin' with their insides on the outsides. I've seen the natives up close. Smelled them, too. They ain't pretty on the eyes, and they sure as shit ain't pretty on the noses. I can't smell 'em anymore. Been here too long, I reckon. They own the mountains this side of the creek."

"So what you're saying," Kasper said, "is that I oughtn't shoot you dead where you stand because we're the only two people who can stop the people of Grave Hollow from killing Della Templeton and using her blood to wake the Sleeper and—destroy the world?"

"Ain't no way her name is Templeton," Rose said. "But yeah, I reckon that about covers it. You can kill me when we're done."

"What's in it for you?" Kasper asked. "Why don't you just run off to someplace else?"

Rose looked at him steady for a long minute. Those eyes had seen some things. The lines on his face, not just the scars, went deep. "I did tell you what they did to my brother, didn't I?"

Kasper nodded. "So it's revenge, is it?"

"Call it spite," Rose said. "Whatever it is they want, I don't want them to have it."

Kasper nodded. That was good enough for him. He glanced outside. He couldn't see down the far side of the pyramid to where Della had fallen, but Morton Stapleton, the sheriff, and the *brujo* guide were racing down those stairs to catch up to her and everyone else seemed to be stepping aside, even if that meant one or two unwittingly slipping off the stairs and down the stone side of the pyramid.

"You've been here a time," Kasper said. "How do we get to her before they do?"

LA CASA DEL DIABLO

CHAPTER 33

Midnight came and went. Morton Stapleton felt the change of day in his bones. The earth aligned with the moon, with other planets, with other celestial objects he couldn't fathom. The time for the blood sacrifice was now, but the daughter of sleeping gods had managed to slip away from the altar and deeper into La Casa del Diablo.

It didn't matter. Blood was blood. Ceremony was for the appreciation of those on hand to witness, the sheriff and *brujo* and other townsfolk of Grave Hollow. The Sleeper cared nothing for the knots used in tying her. It didn't matter if the first cut was to a carotid or radial artery. And it didn't matter if she was presented on the table at the top of the pyramid or anywhere else.

All that mattered was that the blood was warm, and that it was the blood of a relation. Of all the people on earth, there were probably a dozen scattered amongst coastal towns on every ocean.

He and her father, her actual father, had gone to extreme lengths to make sure it would be her.

If he thought he would hit her from that height, he could've shot her from the top of the pyramid. But he had to wait until the alignment. The writings he'd seen in Providence described complicated mechanics under the grounds of the city, wherein certain pipes would swing into place only when the alignment happened.

He could just as easily have descended below the pyramid, found the Sleeper, and spilled her blood there.

She didn't even have to die.

But the people of Grave Hollow expected that. They intended to pass around her flesh and each consume a little bit believing the Sleeper would then spare them.

Morton had intended to have a taste of her tongue. Just to be safe.

The sheriff and *brujo* followed him down the side of the pyramid. He would send them around one side and go around the other himself. They would catch her whichever way she went. They could count on the natives to prevent her from fleeing deeper into La Casa del Diablo.

At the bottom of the steps, more of the townsfolk stepped aside to allow them to do whatever they were doing. From here, they wouldn't have seen Della dive over the other side, but they knew their people.

"You go around that way," Morton said.

The *brujo* guide went immediately, without question. The sheriff, however, said, "I go with you."

Morton didn't argue. It didn't matter. He and the sheriff were here for the same reason. Awaken the Sleeper. End the endless dream.

Going around the side of the pyramid wouldn't be easy. If they went at a run, they would tire themselves out pretty quickly. The uneven terrain off the road proved difficult to navigate. Rocky and broken even at the pyramid's base, it was also steeply cut against the vertical side of the mountain.

"Can we go through?" Morton asked.

"I've been to the top of that pyramid a dozen times," the sheriff told him, "but I reckon the natives would never have let me through the mountains."

Maybe they wouldn't now, either. Morton didn't bother to say so.

The side of the mountain had either been sheared to make room for the pyramid or it had grown beside the structure. Whichever had happened, it gave them no flat surface to traverse the length of the pyramid.

He'd been surprised when Della survived the fall.

"She's a volatile one," the sheriff said. "Hysteria, I suspect, though I'm no doctor."

"Doesn't matter what else she's got," Morton said. "Her mother slept, and sleeps, under the ocean."

He had to use his hands on the side of the mountain to make it possible to walk. He could almost reach some of the lowest mountain windows, but the entrances into the mountain seemed to have gone only as far as the pyramid.

His feet slipped several times. There was no getting any purchase on the side of the pyramid.

"She won't ruin this," the sheriff said. He somehow still carried his gun and walked with the surety of a mountain goat, using only one hand to steady himself against the mountain. "I reckon all we need to do is put a bullet in her brain." He grinned. "Then cut her up and feed. Don't matter none to me if not all the townsfolk are able to make it down before the Sleeper rises."

Didn't matter any to Morton, either.

CHAPTER 34

Della made her way toward the square. Raised slightly over the streets of the city, none of the buildings touched it. She didn't consider it high ground, or in any way safe, but it was the only place she knew the men of Grave Hollow wouldn't reach and the only place she hadn't yet seen the natives.

They watched her silently from their windows and from the streets. They unnerved her, but they didn't seem anxious to chase her. Maybe they knew there was no place for her to run. Maybe they knew she had two bullets in her Derringer that wouldn't do her a lot of good when the sheriff and his people caught up to her. Maybe they knew Morton Stapleton would catch up to her before long.

What did she think she would do, run all the way back to Grave Hollow and the New Mexico Territories? All of that was behind her now. She would never see another sunrise and never hear the crash of the ocean against the shore. She would likely never see her father again, but she wouldn't shed a tear over that.

She would miss Kasper Diehl. She was a damn fool, no better than any soiled dove this side of the Mississippi.

The breeze picked up some strength. It wasn't much, but it was warm and it gave her hope. Hope for what, she couldn't say, but it smelled like salt and sand and seaweed. Though she hadn't grown up near the ocean, her father had taken her a few times. She always felt like she belonged there.

She reached the square. Its footprint might've matched the pyramid. A dozen steps climbed to the edge of the square. The streets of the city ran in the cardinal directions from there like dry canals. At the center of the square, she didn't know where else to go. The full moon beamed straight down on her, as though it had reached the center of the earth and she was it. Beyond the moon, she saw wisps of color and light, clouds that somehow shone more brightly than the moon.

Under all that light, Della felt like she was on stage. Once upon a time, she had dreamt of running away, not with a husband but with a troupe of actors. It would've been a hard life for someone raised on a plantation, but it would not have ended with her at the center of La Casa del Diablo trying to figure out which direction led to the easiest death.

CHAPTER 35

When Morton Stapleton and the sheriff finally reached the side of the pyramid, the *brujo* guide stood there waiting with a Colt hanging loosely in his hand.

Seeing him there, Morton paused. The guide grinned and shrugged.

The sheriff stepped forward, pushing around Morton, to get out of the line of fire. He said, "I'm afraid it don't matter none to the Sleeper who does the cutting."

"I reckon not," Morton said with a heavy sigh. The guide lifted his arm almost leisurely, like he had all the time in the world.

There wasn't much time left in the world, but Morton intended to see it to the end and beyond.

He drew his Colt Paterson. He'd had the weapon a while. It had been hanging on his hip the day he found Della in Georgia, but the first time he'd killed a man with it was back in Rhode Island a bunch of years earlier in a library basement. So it was second nature to thumb back the hammer as he lifted the gun, which dropped the trigger into place.

He kept four chambers loaded, leaving the fifth empty so he wouldn't accidentally shoot himself while wearing it. From this distance, there was no chance he would miss, and he put the bullet right in the *brujo* guide's heart before he had bothered to aim his own weapon.

The *brujo* exploded into a dozen black-feathered crows. They scattered with an inhuman scream, swarming past Morton and brushing his face. They scraped his cheek, his throat, and almost got his eyes.

Then they flew away in all directions but especially upward. Only one crow dropped to the ground, the bullet having pierced its heart and nearly ripping one of its wings off. Half the bird's breast remained in place. The rest was pulp floating in the atmosphere.

The sheriff grinned, revealing several missing teeth, removed his hat as he looked away to follow the path of one of the crows. "Never trust a man who sleeps with his eyes open."

Morton pressed the barrel of his Paterson to the sheriff's temple and, with slow deliberation, cocked the hammer. He said, "I'm afraid it don't matter none to the Sleeper who does the cutting."

Then he shot the sheriff.

From here, it seemed unlikely that any of the townsfolk could have seen him, so he returned his weapon to its holster, took a breath, and noted that one of the crows had perched on the side of the mountain.

"Was the only thing to do," Morton told the bird.

None of them had run across Della, which meant either she'd fled into one of the mountains or deeper into the silent and brooding city. A wind had been growing gradually stronger. It struck his face, then traveled the length of the pyramid.

He walked the city's street and followed Della's scent. She had always smelled vibrant and alive. It was a pleasant odor, not overdone like a harlot's perfume or the reek of death. The smell of her overcame the dust, death, and decay that permeated this part of the desert.

It didn't feel like he was walking through a desert town, though. The gray rocks and a tinge of dampness on the air made him think of the northern Atlantic on a winter's night. The full moon had guided him then, and it guided him now.

He found Della at the center of the square. She stared back at him like a lost little lamb.

He gave her a smile. Something like a smile. It probably wasn't any better than Kasper Diehl's, but at least it was honest.

LA CASA DEL DIABLO

CHAPTER 36

Against his better judgement and against every instinct screaming for vengeance, Kasper Diehl followed Damon Rose deeper into the mountain. The path they took intersected others, but Rose seemed to have an idea of where he was leading them.

They didn't jaw. Nothing else needed saying. When this was over, Kasper would still have a bullet with Rose's name on it. The ghosts of his mother, his sister, and his father would rest easy tonight.

He wasn't much of a thinking man. He didn't consider the implications of all the things Rose said. He just knew what was the right thing to do, and that was not to let the girl die.

One of the natives stood in one of the tunnels. It didn't move. It didn't even seem alive. It appeared damp. Ribbons of green and brown clung to its flesh. Its arms were humanlike, but its face lacked familiar features.

It startled him, to see it so close. Rose, ahead of him, paused and said, "Leave it."

Kasper was inclined to do just that. He glanced back over his shoulder. Another of the natives lurked in the murky unnatural iridescence. He didn't see it move, but had heard the squish of its wet feet.

"Leave it," Rose said. "There are worse things."

"Worse?" Kasper asked.

"They live here," Rose said. "They stand. They watch. Sometimes they walk. And sometimes, something else emerges from the shadows to—eat them."

The native's head tilted. It lifted its arm to reach for Kasper. He jumped away, nearly banging into Rose.

"You don't want to be here when the creatures feed. The natives—scream."

The tunnels descended. But they sometimes rose for a while. They switched back and forth frequently. With no windows, Kasper could not judge their elevation. He kept looking back. The natives kept their distance as long as he kept moving forward.

There were more of them now.

They showed no sign of breathing through those gills.

Finally, Rose rounded a corner and they exited the mountain.

The city street here was narrow. They emerged directly across from the doorway to one of the city's low structures. They might have been homes, though the doorway had no actual door. It was large enough for the natives, which seemed generally a foot or two taller than Kasper. One of the natives stood in that doorway.

Damon Rose seemed used to them. He'd been in this place a long time now. Kasper wondered how the man slept at night.

He wondered other things, too.

Things he wouldn't give voice to.

The full moon shone straight above La Casa del Diablo. Rose turned to the left, leading them deeper into the city. From here, there was no place to go but deeper. They were north of the pyramid, moving parallel to it toward the square he'd seen from the mountain.

Once it came into view, Kasper heard voices.

They had to climb stairs to get to the square, Rose indicated with his gun one set, east of the square, while he went to the northern stairs.

LA CASA DEL DIABLO

CHAPTER 37

When Morton Stapleton climbed up to the square, Della's spirits dropped. He drew his gun from its holster though she knew he wouldn't shoot her. He needed her on top of the pyramid, where he would carve her flesh.

"I should've stayed in Georgia," she told him.

"That was never going to be allowed," Morton told her. "Your father and I had—an arrangement. He would've married you to me, if necessary."

"You wouldn't have touched me," she said.

He shrugged. "And I never did. If that's what I wanted, there were plenty of fancy women and fast tricks wanting to earn a dollar or two in the desert."

She found it difficult to hold onto her fury. She'd had a hundred chances to kill Morton in his sleep. She never had to come to Grave Hollow. She might've poisoned his coffee back in El Paso and headed north. She could've gone to Denver City, or back to New Orleans The Mississippi had been as much a home to her as the Atlantic.

She felt obliged to reserve some of that anger for her father.

"What if it didn't work?" she asked.

"A thousand thousand years more, then, they might wait," Morton said, "but you'd be dead, and I might as well live out the last of my days here in Grave Hollow."

"They never would've let you."

Morton shrugged. "The sheriff's dead. I don't think anyone else in Grave Hollow will be much of a bother to me."

A crow landed with a caw in the middle of the square, nearer to Della than to Morton. She realized they'd been circling each other. She nodded toward the Paterson in his hand. "You won't use that."

"I fear you may have lost your nerve."

She had to turn to look up to the top of the pyramid. It dominated the city. Faces of Grave Hollow stared back down at her.

At her level, however, Kasper Diehl rose into view. He climbed the same steps Morton had used. He held his gun. A surge of emotion confused her. If he hadn't interrupted them on their way to Grave Hollow, she would've given her blood to ancient and unknowable gods without a second thought.

She wore a series of bruises, scrapes, and cuts that would scar instead.

Kasper walked to his left to get a line on Morton Stapleton without having to go through her. Another man climbed the stairs behind her. She didn't recognize him, but assumed his name was Damon Rose.

The three men formed a kind of triangle around her. She found herself closest to Morton. They all had weapons drawn.

Della drew her Derringer with her left hand and hated herself for pointing it at Kasper Diehl.

CHAPTER 38

So this was how it would be.

Della pointed the Derringer Kasper had given her back at him. Her aim didn't look to be too steady. Stapleton's Paterson wavered only because he didn't know if Damon Rose or Kasper Diehl was the greater threat to him.

Damon Rose kept his Paterson, the same weapon he'd used to kill Kasper's father, steady on Stapleton. Despite being a murderer, he wasn't ready to see the world end.

The moon burned above them.

Natives watched from their windows.

The wind swirled around them.

Slowly, Kasper shifted his aim from Stapleton to Rose. Whatever else happened tonight, it was his duty to deliver Damon Rose to the vengeful ghosts that had haunted Kasper since he was eight. The smell of that Paterson's gunpowder when Rose turned it on Kasper as a boy never left him. It never would. Even with Rose dead and buried, that smell would follow him to his grave.

He looked from one man to the other, Rose and Stapleton, two men whose wicked agendas had caused them to cross Kasper's path. He couldn't help but see Della's eyes as he swept his gaze across the field. Her

Derringer trembled. A tear had dropped from her eye and cleaned a path down the dirt and dust on her cheek.

It came to this. What kind of man was he? He had been driven by vengeance for so long, he'd never had an opportunity for other motivations. He might love a woman like Della. She might shoot him where he stood. But nothing would return his mother. She'd died on the ranch almost twenty years ago and the dust had claimed her corpse. His sister, too, resided six feet under a marker with her name on it.

Only Kasper's father remained. He remained in the Walker Colt.

Slowly, Kasper bent to one knee and laid his father to rest on the eastern edge of the square in La Casa del Diablo. It wasn't the best final resting place, but perhaps it would give his father's ghost the peace he deserved in death.

Just as slowly, he rose back to his feet.

That left Stapleton and Rose aiming their weapons at each other and Della looking confused. She tried to give him a smile. It wasn't much of a thing.

She spun and fired the Derringer. More gunshots followed: the Patersons, each echoing like the thunder of gods.

Della's bullet hit Stapleton in the shoulder. He spun only enough that his own shot went wide and missed his mark. Damon Rose, however, did not miss. The first shot put a hole between Stapleton's eyes. It came out the other side of his skull. Rose's second shot hit his throat.

Damon Rose's third shot was meant for Kasper. No man, bandit, bastard, or banker, should have lowered his weapon to give someone like Rose his life.

But he never got the third shot off. Della had one more bullet in that Derringer and sent it in his direction. It ripped into the side of his throat.

Kasper had the Peacemaker he'd picked up in the desert, and his hand was true. The first .45 caliber cartridge found Damon Rose's heart and exposed it to the world. The second and third were close, putting a good series of holes in Rose's chest. The fourth and fifth shots hit Rose's chest just below the throat and his face just below the eye.

The gunfire echoed through the city of La Casa del Diablo.

Kasper didn't fire the last cartridge.

He returned the weapon to its holster. He liked the feel of it. This, he would keep for the rest of his life. He felt no need to say any words for his father, so he stepped over the Walker and went to Della.

She fell into his arms.

He held her and kissed her and said, "I reckon we ought to get out of this damned place before the sun rises."

She smiled. "I reckon you're right, Mr. Diehl."

They left the square. Natives watched from their windows and from the streets, and they parted to allow Kasper and Della to walk by. They went to the side of the pyramid. They made their way carefully over the steep stone incline alongside the mountain wall. When they reached the far end, the townsfolk of Grave Hollow remained on the pyramid steps. They watched, and at least one sobbed visibly.

Kasper and Della walked east. Toward the coming sunrise.

CHAPTER 39

Della, whose father's surname was Devereux, had not broken any bones on her fall down the side of the pyramid. But she had gained numerous scrapes and scratches and cuts, all of which had left blood on the surface of the stone. The blood didn't run fast, but one drop found its way through a tiny crevice in the pyramid.

The men of Grave Hollow had been prepared to spill every drop of Della's blood, but only one was necessary.

It fell through the crevice and hit the skin of the Sleeper.

The earth trembled as the Sleeper roused from its slumber.

The pyramid crumbled.

The townsfolk of Grave Hollow fell from the steps and fell from the altar. Some tumbled down the sides of the pyramid, but many fell straight into the massive cavern below. Some were still falling when the Sleeper rose, shattering the rest of the pyramid.

Far to the east, down the long road that led back to Grave Hollow, Kasper Diehl and Della Devereux had reached the creek when the earth shuddered and rumbled. They looked back to see the ten thousand eyes and the ten thousand mouths and the ten thousand tongues of the Sleeper. It rose to a height taller than the mountains and stretched ten thousand tentacles or arms or appendages that defied description. Maybe it felt the first rays of sunlight as dawn struggled to break over the eastern horizon.

The Sleeper ceased its dreaming.

end

ACKNOWLEDGMENTS

I wrote this tale during the earliest and darkest months of the pandemic while hiding from the world at my sister's house. Jeneine, her husband Chuck, and her son Jacob ("The Baritone") were good enough to give me space to work on this and other projects while the world outside our doors ended.

I must thank Morgan for being the kind of friend I needed when I most needed one, without whom none of this would have been possible.

Thank you to Sean (of the Madrid Writer's Club) for getting me into westerns in the first place, and Joshua and the ghostwriting gig for helping facilitating that.

As always, a special thanks to Sabine and the Rose Fairy. You will always be with me.

ABOUT THE AUTHOR

John Urbancik isn't old enough to have lived in the west of *La Casa del Diablo*, but he has seen the sun set over the desert in the west and walked through those mountains.

In addition to books of poetry and a nonfiction book based on his podcast *Inkstains*, Urbancik has written books like the *DarkWalker* series, *Stale Reality* (also available in Russian), *Once Upon a Time in Midnight*, and the collection *The Museum of Curiosities*.

Born on a small island in the northeast United States called Manhattan, he is currently sequestered in an undisclosed location in the woods of Pennsylvania near the Susquehanna River.

ALSO BY JOHN URBANCIK

NOVELS
Sins of Blood and Stone
Breath of the Moon
Once Upon a Time in Midnight
Stale Reality
The Corpse and the Girl from Miami
DarkWalker 1: Hunting Grounds
DarkWalker 2: Inferno
DarkWalker 3: The Deep City
DarkWalker 4: Armageddon
DarkWalker 5: Ghost Stories
DarkWalker 6: Other Realms

NOVELLAS
A Game of Colors
The Rise and Fall of Babylon (with Brian Keene)
Wings of the Butterfly
House of Shadow and Ash
Necropolis
Quicksilver
Beneath Midnight
Zombies vs. Aliens vs. Robots vs. Cowboys vs.
Ninja vs. Investment Bankers vs. Green Berets
Colette and the Tiger

COLLECTIONS
Shadows, Legends & Secrets
Sound and Vision
Tales of the Fantastic and the Phantasmagoric
The Museum of Curiosities

POETRY
John the Revelator
Odyssey

NONFICTION
InkStained: On Creativity, Writing, and Art

INKSTAINS
Multiple volumes

Made in the USA
Coppell, TX
12 February 2023

12715775R00094